About the Author

Lana McAra is an award-winning, international best-selling author and ghostwriter of forty titles with half a million books sold (many under the name Rosey Dow), including two cookbooks. An author via traditional publishing for twenty-five years, she won the national Christy Award, The Literary Titan Silver Book Award, and also The Book Excellence Award finalist for *Reaping the Whirlwind*. Visit her website at www.LanaMcAra.com for her schedule of speaking engagements and new releases. "Lana teaches an 8-module course to beginning novelists. Find out more at http://HowToWriteANovelThatSells.com"

Lana McAra

The Englewood Medium: Shaken but Not Stirred

Scott
Π

Linda — sister — Haley — — best friend Barb

Daylon
= neighbor
downstairs

Olympia Publishers
London

www.olympiapublishers.com
OLYMPIA PAPERBACK EDITION

A CIP catalogue record for th
available from the British

ISBN: 978-1-80439-3

First Published in 2023

Olympia Publishers
Tallis House
2 Tallis Street
London
EC4Y 0AB

Printed in Great Britain

Chapter One

Haley Meyers stepped in front of the burly moving man before he reached the outside stairs to her second-floor apartment. She firmly grasped the antique Martha Washington sewing cabinet in his hands and took it from him. "I'll take care of this."

It was two feet wide and lightweight. She had picked it up plenty of times. Given to Haley by her grandmother, the table was more than one hundred years old. Even though it was shrink-wrapped, she was still afraid of getting it scratched.

"Need some help with that?" Daylon Jasper called as he lightly descended the steps. Her new downstairs neighbor had a full head of gray hair, but still managed to seem like a kid. Maybe it was that ironic glint in his blue eyes.

Haley leaned back a little as she hitched the small table higher to clear the bottom step. "I'm okay. Thanks."

The men retreated to the truck. Her shrink-wrapped sofa had their full attention.

Haley had rented the upstairs of a wide two-story house with an apartment on each level. Each unit had its own verandah, a Southern style unusual in northern Pennsylvania.

At the landing where the stairs turned left, the toe of Haley's sneaker caught on the step. She lurched forward. Her hands flew out to grab the railing.

The table bounced down the stairs and landed in a heap. One of the legs had broken off and poked through the ripped plastic. One side of the table had a deep gash.

Unable to move, Haley sat on a step and stared down at the disaster. *What was she thinking?* For a long moment, she couldn't breathe.

Her sister, Linda Blankenship, appeared at the top of the stairs. She gasped. "Haley! What did you do?"

Haley shook her head. She had no words.

"Grandma's table!" Linda burst out as she brushed past Haley. She knelt down for a closer look, then glared up her sister. "What a crock! How could you be so stupid?"

Sighing heavily, Haley joined her. Both women were blond and forty-something with the classy aura of career women. Linda was a medical doctor and Haley a psychologist. That's where their similarities ended. Linda had the taut body and edgy vibe of an athlete—which she was. Haley liked to say she loved her soft curves—which she did.

Daylon called out, "I know a guy who can fix that. I'll text you his number." As the two movers positioned the sofa on the electric lift, Daylon grabbed two boxes from the sidewalk and headed up the stairs.

Haley slowly shook her head. "I guess that takes care of that," she said.

Muttering under her breath, Linda picked up the broken table leg. Haley bent down to carefully gather the plastic around the fragments of wood, so none would fall out.

Working with the ease of people who have been together forever, they carefully placed everything in the trunk of Haley's car and headed back inside.

"Anyone care for a drink?" Haley asked when she reached the front door. She looked into the fridge. "I've got cherry, raspberry and orange electrolyte drinks, iced tea, cola..." She glanced at her sister. "...or wine."

Linda grimaced and let out a deep sigh. "Too early, sad to say."

Haley tried to give Linda's outbursts a pass. With a busy medical practice and three kids, Dr. Linda was always exhausted and on her last nerve.

Haley passed around beverage bottles, then looked for a place to perch. Everything was wrapped in plastic. Finally, she sat on the floor with her back against the living room wall and took a long drink of peach tea.

A minute later, the sofa made its way into the room, and she was back on her feet giving directions.

For the past four years, Haley had lived in a five-bedroom house-share across town. Professional women came and went almost monthly. They were cordial to each other, and the arrangement worked. One day, two of her housemates had a disagreement over the fridge that soon launched into a full-out feud. Neither of them was willing to end it by either apologizing or leaving.

Finally, Haley had enough and started looking for another place. With a small trust fund left to her by her father as well as income from her counseling practice, she could well afford her own apartment. She was in a house share because she didn't want to live alone. Now, living alone was her top priority.

When she told her friends at the Healing Circle that she was looking for an apartment, Sonia Summers told her this upstairs unit was under renovations and would soon be available. Fresh and gleaming, one bedroom and one bath, minutes from her office—Haley couldn't ask for better. The only drawback was the stairs, but Daylon seemed eager to help, so that worked out, too.

Linda's husband, Scott, and Daylon pushed furniture around to Haley's satisfaction. Unpacking photos, Linda turned one toward Haley. It was their parents' wedding photo. They were both gone now. "Where do you want this one?"

"How about a grouping in the hall?" Haley said. "Set the photos in a row along the wall, and I'll put them up later."

Linda lifted a stack of gold frames. The top picture showed Haley's son at his college graduation, squinting into the sun next to Haley and her daughter, the older of the two.

An hour later, Daylon paused next to Haley. He waited while she pressed her house key across a line of packing tape and pulled the top of the box open.

"I've got to run. If you need anything, text me."

She smiled. "I appreciate the help, Daylon. Thank you."

He put his two fingers to his temple in a loose salute and left.

As he strode past the wide living room window, Linda whispered to Haley, "Wow, I'd say you lucked out."

Haley looked doubtful. "Sonia told me he's a retired Marine officer. He's probably used to barking orders. Not my type. At all." Haley's phone chirped. She glanced at it.

"What's that?" Linda asked.

"It's a notice from SeniorsMeetup.com. Eli Loomis, the guy I've been dating, just messaged me."

"C'mon. Let's see him."

Haley touched the screen a few times, then showed her an image of a shirtless bald guy with a giant gut. He was holding up a fish.

Linda's lips twisted. "And you'll take that instead of the hunk right under your feet?"

"There's more to think about than looks," Haley said. "Like loyalty."

Linda's mouth tightened. Before she could reply, Scott came out of the bathroom. Haley slid her phone into the back pocket of her jeans.

"Are you ready?" he asked Linda. He had a perfect jawline and an effortless swoosh to the front lock of his dark hair.

Linda put her hand on her stomach and groaned. "I'm starving. Let's get some supper." She grabbed her purse off the table. "We'll be back!" she told Haley, and they headed out the door.

As they passed her bare front window, they waved at her. Suddenly feeling exposed, Haley decided her next task was to cover that window with a curtain. She didn't want to sleep in here with it wide open like that.

Digging through the jumble in one corner of the living room, she found the bundle of curtain rods. Her electric screwdriver lay on the table, and the stepladder was in the kitchen. She'd have this done before they came back.

On the second screw, she hit something behind the wallboard. No matter how hard she pressed, the screw spun in place. Sweating and frustrated, she imagined the wasted time and expense of hiring a handyman for such a small task. When it came to things like this, Scott was useless. She wouldn't even ask him.

Asking Daylon for help with something this trivial would be humiliating. She was not a helpless female. She'd rather hire someone. To put in a screw? *C'mon!*

Suddenly, she felt her father's warmth around her. She had a burst of strength in her right shoulder, and the screw went straight in. She felt Dad's satisfied smile, like he used to smile when one of his endless projects came out perfect.

Whoa. What just happened?

Holding the screwdriver, she came down the ladder, took two steps back and sat in a chair.

"That was easy." Her dad mellow voice sounded clear and strong.

She gasped and jerked around to see him leaning against the wall, grinning at her. He was younger, like he looked when she was in grade school, thirty years ago.

She stared at him, her mind completely blank. She must be going crazy. Even crazier, she wasn't the least bit scared.

"Sorry to startle you," he said. "I didn't know how to do this without causing a scene."

"You're wearing your Penn State shirt," she gasped.

He looked down. "It's my favorite."

"But... do ghosts have closets?"

"I prefer *disembodied spirit*," he said, then he threw his head back and laughed, exactly the way he used to. Exactly the sound she had missed so much these past four years. She had an urge to jump up and hug him, but she stayed rooted in the chair.

He took a seat on the sofa. "Finally, you moved near an electrical substation, and I can pull enough energy to show myself to you."

"Where were you in the meantime?"

"I've always been with you and your sister, but not really with you. It's complicated. Let's just say, I'm glad to be here."

"What about Linda? Have you shown yourself to her?"

He shook his head. "She doesn't believe. I don't want to scare her into a nervous breakdown."

"And you're not scaring me?" Haley felt heat rising in her throat. "Dad. I just about passed out."

"But you didn't, Haley my girl. You didn't."

At that moment, Linda appeared in the front window carrying brown paper bags. Haley looked up to return her wave. When she looked back at the sofa, Dad was gone.

14

Linda bustled in. "Scott dropped me off and took dinner to the kids." They had three children, all currently in middle school.

As she unpacked food cartons, Linda glanced at Haley still seated in the chair. "What's going on?"

"I just saw Dad."

Linda's eyes narrowed. Instantly she transformed from a helpful sister into a family physician.

"He was right there..." Haley nodded toward the sofa. "...talking to me."

"I'm giving you a referral to a neurologist," Linda said, pulling a pen light from the side pocket of her purse. "How long has this been going on? Do you have double vision, dizziness?" She bent over Haley, shining the light into her eyes.

Haley pulled away and put up her hand.

"I'm serious!" Linda said. "You have to get checked."

"No, I don't. I must have dozed off, and it was a dream."

"Has this happened before?" Linda demanded.

"No." Haley stood to end the conversation. "What did you bring? Let's eat."

The subject dropped, and Haley didn't pick it up again. After they finished eating shrimp fried rice, Linda helped put up the living room curtain, and they called it a night.

As far as Haley was concerned, once she had emptied her suitcase and located the coffee pot, she could take her time in unpacking the rest.

Monday morning, Haley left a few minutes early for the office. She had a therapy practice at Alexion Acupuncture on State Street, the central avenue in Englewood. That meant she rented a room and shared a receptionist with several other practitioners. She was on her own for building her client base. Over the years, she had developed a referral network of medical doctors, coaches and energy healing practitioners who handed out her cards. Most of her clients came from them.

A high school science teacher for ten years, Haley completed her first Master's degree in education and her second Master's degree in psychology. She passed her boards on the first try and opened a therapy practice shortly afterward. That was six years ago.

Digging into her leather shoulder bag to locate her chirping phone, she stepped outside her front door and locked it. She finally found the phone and glanced at the screen. A tiny red heart blinked in the top left corner. Someone on SeniorsMeetup.com wanted to meet her.

"Your boyfriend texting you?" a deep voice called from below her porch railing. Daylon peered up at her with a teasing grin.

She pressed her lips together to squelch the smile filling her mouth. "And that is your business, why?" she asked. She carefully planted her foot on the first step down.

"Good morning to you, too." He went to the back of his blue pickup truck and opened the tailgate. He wore a red buffalo-plaid jacket. Daylon was the brother-in-law of Martin and Sonia Summers, who owned this property, although Haley wasn't clear whether he was related to Martin or Sonia.

Haley's pumps clicked on the wooden steps. Her black skirt felt tight around her knees. Inside her car, she paused to take a quick peek at her new prospect on SeniorsMeetup, someone calling himself YoMyMama.

Online dating had become like a gambling game to her—tantalizing and addictive. You never knew when you'd hit a triple and win big. Or something like that. So far, she couldn't get lucky, but she kept trying. Why not?

YoMyMama happened to be a guy on a motorcycle with a blue bandana tied around his head and a bleary look in his eye. She put her phone down and turned the key in the ignition.

Nothing happened.

What?

She tried again.

Nothing.

How could that be? The car was working fine last night. She'd come home from her date around eight o'clock. If you could call that a date. Actually, it was a break-up dinner, followed by a quick escape.

She rolled down her window and called to Daylon, "Can I ask you a favor?"

He came around the side of the truck. "What's the trouble?"

"My car is dead."

"You don't say." He came closer. "Try it again, so I can hear what happens."

She turned the key. Silence. "I just did," she said. "It doesn't make a sound."

"Can you pop the hood?" he asked.

She bit back a smart answer and found the button under the dashboard.

Two minutes later, he came to her window. "It's the battery."

She didn't believe him. "I just replaced it last winter."

"I have jumper cables in my truck. Ten minutes, and you'll be on your way."

She tapped her fingers on the soft steering wheel cover. A dead battery could mean a lot of hidden problems. She'd have to get a mechanic to check it out. Since she became single, at the first sign of car trouble she didn't let one day go by before taking her car to the shop.

When she told Daylon she wanted to drop the car off, he said, "I'll follow you and take you to your office." He disappeared under the hood. "Try it now," he called.

The engine roared to life. So did the headlights.

Daylon removed the cables and dropped the hood into place.

"I know I didn't leave the lights on," Haley told him.

He nodded. "They were off when I came in around nine o'clock."

He looked at his blackened hands. "Give me a minute to wash up, and I'll be right with you."

Englewood, Pennsylvania, (population 8,486) had three auto repair shops. One of them was just down the street, so dropping off the car was a quick process. Going most places in Englewood was a quick process.

Haley and Daylon barely spoke during her time in his truck. In less than ten minutes, he pulled into the lot behind her office building. He gave her a quick nod as she closed her door, and his truck disappeared down the street.

Haley headed to the back door of her office. In less than ten minutes, Flo Yeager would be coming through the door.

A single mom in her mid-thirties, Flo became a client after a disastrous year completely dismantled her life. First, she lost her sixteen-year-old son Freddy to a terminal kidney disease, followed by a nasty divorce and custody battle over Fleeta, Freddy's twin sister. Flo and her ex ended up with joint custody. In their case, the fight never stopped. Sometimes Fleeta came with her mother for sessions, and once Fleeta had come alone. Poor kid. She had been through a rough time, too.

Once inside the building, Haley drew up when she spotted Flo sitting on a loveseat in the waiting room. Her sleek black hair hung half out of its clip. Her makeup was sliding off from crying.

Haley hurried to her.

She had heavy dark shadows under her swollen eyes. When she caught sight of Haley, she gasped, "Pauly..." and lost her breath in a sob. Pauly was Flo's boyfriend. Haley had met him twice when he dropped Flo off for her appointment. He usually left Flo in the waiting room, then strolled down State Street while she had her session.

Haley reached for her. "Let's get you settled on the sofa, and I'll make you some tea, okay?"

Pressing a wad of tissues to her face, Flo nodded.

Twenty minutes went by before Flo calmed down enough to talk. Haley pulled out her secret recipe for calming a meltdown—lotion-filled tissues, a pink furry throw and hot tea.

With Flo quietly sipping tea, Haley kept her body language relaxed in her wingback chair. She had her yellow legal pad on her lap. "What started this whole thing?" she asked gently.

"Yesterday afternoon, I told him it was over." Flo murmured. "For real this time." She drew in a shaky breath. "I told him he couldn't come around my place anymore."

"How did he take that?"

Flo brushed at her right cheek and left a wet streak. Even with mascara over half her face, she had that magic something women spend thousands of dollars to achieve and still fall short of.

Her voice wavered. "First he screamed at me... then he started crying and peeled out of the cul-de-sac in his truck." She rubbed above her left eyebrow. "A couple of my neighbors came to their windows." She winced and more tears flowed. "Humiliating."

Flo's hectic relationship with Pauly Hammond had taken up most of their sessions for the past six months. They made a cute couple, both of them about 5'2", with olive complexions and dark hair, like two peas in a pod. Pauly adored Flo, but they couldn't seem to resolve their conflicts. Over the past six months, Flo had broken up with him three or four times, then a few days later she'd take him back.

After all this lovely, sensitive woman had been through, Haley wished so much that Flo would end the chaos. However, Flo was in the driver's seat. It was her life. Haley could only offer suggestions and support. Flo had to do the rest.

Snuggled into a corner of the sofa, Flo sipped tea. "It's for real this time, Haley. I need to get settled down and start a new life where I can be who I want to be." More tears. "I love Pauly. I really love him… but he's not good for me. He keeps everything stirred up, and I can't get stabilized."

Haley nodded. "You're a strong woman, Flo. You're smart enough to know what's good for you, and you have the courage to follow through."

Flo's mouth pulled sideways. "I feel like a bawling kindergartner." She yanked three tissues from the box next to her and made a wide swipe across her face as though wiping away her grief. When she sat back, she had a look of quiet resolve where the pain had been before. "I have to do this. It's my life, and I'm taking it back. I have to for…Fleeta's sake."

Haley nodded. "Here…" From her desk drawer, she pulled a round black stone with *Power* engraved on it. "I picked this up when I was at the shore last year for a time like this."

Flo took the stone from her and rolled it in her hand, looking at it from every angle, feeling its smooth surface.

"That's who you are, Flo. Powerful." Haley set her notepad aside. "Are you ready to rest back and close your eyes?"

Placing her cup on the coffee table, Flo nodded. For the next twenty minutes, Haley led her through a calming and clearing meditation.

When the timer on Haley's desk sounded, Flo collected her wadded tissues and dropped them into the tiny wastebin nearby. She said, "Next week I'm going to visit my brother in Bayard. I'll have to miss that session and pick up in two weeks."

Haley made the correction to the online calendar. She pulled a book from her shelf. "Here's something for you to read in the meantime."

Flo opened the front cover showing Haley's business card taped inside. "I'll get it back to you when I come in next time," she said.

Haley stood, signaling the end of the session. "Email me if you need me," she said.

"Thank you, Haley. I don't know what I'd do without you."

Smiling gently, Haley watched until she exited the back door, then she opened her laptop to write up her notes. Her next client was due to arrive in ten minutes—another woman with an abusive, controlling husband. If not for her own calming and clearing process, Haley would have never lasted this long as a counselor. So much pain...

Chapter Two

Shortly before noon, Haley was at her office desk typing patient files when a gentle knock sounded at her door. Scooting the rolling desk chair and leaning to the right, she turned the knob and opened it to see a cloud of fluffy red hair.

"Hi, Cheri," she said, pushing the door wide open before scooting back to her desk.

Cherie Alexion owned this office building. She had an ethereal presence and sort of floated along instead of connecting to solid earth like regular people did. Today, she had on a flowing white skirt with a flowing white tunic, all cotton muslin and a fringe dangling from every edge.

Alexion Acupuncture offered acupuncture, Chinese medicine, crystal healing, aromatherapy and a host of other things, but most of all Cheri was a tapped-in, turned-on psychic. She swished inside and brought the smell of blended essential oils with her. "I'm heading over to the Healing Circle," she said. "Are you ready?"

Haley pulled the top of her laptop down. "More than ready," she said, grabbing her yellow shoulder bag. It was big enough to hold her laptop, although she rarely took the computer out of the office. She'd rather lock it into a filing cabinet.

"What's the matter?" Cheri asked, looking at Haley more closely. "You look a little stressed."

"I do have a story to tell," Haley replied, "but I'll tell it to everyone at once." She led the way toward the back exit. "My stomach is getting cranky. I wonder what leftover goodies Barb has for us today. I haven't seen her all weekend. She's been catering a wedding."

Every Wednesday at noon, the Healing Circle met in the back room of A Summer Place, the bookstore across the back alley from Alexion.

Sonia and Martin had opened A Summer Place twenty-five years ago and had managed to keep the store thriving despite the massive popularity of Kindle and Audible. Now retirement age, the Martins were still going full speed ahead.

Crossing the alley, Haley and Cheri entered the back entrance of the bookstore and took an immediate right into the meeting room.

The makeshift kitchen area had a long counter holding a microwave, hotplate and coffee maker with an ancient fridge in the corner. On the other side of the room, two green vinyl sofas faced each other—upcycled from a teacher's lounge.

At the counter stood Haley's best friend and the town's most popular caterer, Barb Morales, unpacking foil containers from a large thermal case. Barb was small, Cuban and all business. She had tied a red-and-blue silk scarf as a headband with a messy bun showing from the top of it. She wore a white chef's coat and blazing red lipstick.

Barb and Haley had been best friends since third grade. Barb was the real reason Haley moved to Englewood four years ago, although Linda didn't know that.

"Hey, Baby Barby," Haley said, giving her a sideways hug. "What's on the menu today?"

"Lots of mac-and-cheese, a little sliced beef, and a ton of broccoli salad." Barb glanced up. "Hi, Cheri," she said.

Cheri looked over the spread. "Anything a vegan can eat?"

In one swift move, Barb dived into her bag and pulled out a Chinese food carton. "I saved you some tabbouleh," she said, triumphant. "Just in the nick of time, too. Someone on the cleanup crew had her eye on this, but I nabbed it for you." She handed the carton to Cheri, who happily plucked a metal fork from the nearby rack and headed to her favorite spot on a sofa.

Haley smiled inside. Typical Barb, remembering what people loved.

"I'm starving!" Haley grabbed a plate and didn't hold back in piling on the mac-and-cheese.

Two more members arrived and lined up to fill plates. Everyone looked forward to the leftovers from Barb's events. They munched in contented silence for a few minutes, then Cheri opened the meeting by saying, "Haley has something to tell us."

Barb grinned. "Don't tell me. You're sure he's The One."

"Actually, we had The Breakup Talk."

Sympathetic moans all around.

"What happened?" Barb asked, always eager for the down-and-dirty details.

"That's old news," Haley said, with a wave. "The real news is that my dad showed up in my living room."

"What?" Barb gasped. She glanced at Cheri. "He died four years ago."

Immediately, she had everyone's full attention. Haley gave an overview of what happened, ending with, "He said he has to stay within range of the power station in order to appear. I didn't understand it."

Cheri nodded. "Non-physical humans can draw energy from electricity. That's why they often appear in homes near large powerlines."

"Where does he go when he's not visible?" Haley asked.

"He's still around, maybe fully conscious of everything or maybe not. I'm not sure about that myself."

"I haven't seen him since then," Haley said. "Maybe he just popped in to say hello and that's it."

Cheri closed her eyes for a second. "He's watching over you," she said. "You might not see him all the time, but he's watching over you."

The meeting moved into the healing phase where everyone takes a turn at receiving help from the group. The Healing Circle had provided Haley with a place to clear away the worries and weights of both her practice and her life. She only missed Healing Circle meetings if she had to be out of town.

At the end of the meeting, Cheri called out, "Don't forget, tomorrow night—Naked Yoga."

Everyone laughed. Two years ago, Sonia Summers had started a women-over-fifty hot yoga class at Alexion. Shortly afterward, she remarked to the group that it should be called Naked Yoga, because everyone ended up pulling off their clothes by the time class was over. From that point on, hot yoga became Naked Yoga to the Healing Circle. Haley wasn't into yoga.

After the meeting, Barb met Haley outside the back door. "So, you had The Breakup Talk?"

Haley nodded. "It wasn't cordial. He showed me how right I was to call it quits. End of story."

Barb handed over the remaining mac-and-cheese.

Haley hefted the foil pan, gauging the weight of it. "I won't be able to finish this in a week."

Barb laughed and moved toward the alley. "Rumor has it, you have a handsome man in the apartment downstairs. He won't refuse to share it with you. Will he?" Walking backwards, she laughed at Haley's dismayed expression. "Call me!"

Shaking her head and chuckling in spite of herself, Haley picked up her phone to call Linda. The blabbermouth.

Later that afternoon, a text from the garage gave her good news. Her car was fine. She could come and pick it up.

After her last client, Haley paused in the doorway of Cheri's office. "Do you have time to give me a ride to the garage? I need to pick up my car."

Cheri came out of her seat with a wide smile. "Of course." She gave Haley's arm a playful pat. "I knew you were one of us! So, your father showed up to chat, did he?"

"Scared the living crap out of me. I told my sister Linda, and she thought I was hallucinating. She was shining a light in my eyes in less than ten seconds."

"It's a gift," Cheri said. "An honor."

"Is he watching me in the bathroom? What if I decide to have an overnight guest sometime? What then?" Haley flexed her shoulders. "It's creepy, Cheri. Admit it. It's creepy."

With a knowing look, Cheri chuckled and reached for her purse. "You'll get used to it."

Twenty minutes later, Cheri dropped Haley off at the shop. Soon afterward, Haley arrived home, eager to kick off her shoes and enjoy a cold wine spritzer.

Her apartment had a simple layout with a central hall. The bedroom and ensuite bath were on the right with their door toward the back of the apartment. The open concept living room and kitchen were on the left with the wide doorway near the small entry.

Her soft sofa had a floral pattern with wide arms and a rounded back. It had found its home beneath the wide living room window with a lounge chair at its left and a low coffee table in front. An oval dining table took up a large part of the central area with the kitchen along the back wall.

Haley was at the kitchen counter with her back toward the room, pouring Riesling into a glass when Dad's voice came from the living area. "Hard day at the office?"

Startled, she managed to set down the bottle without spilling before she turned around. He was sitting in the lounge chair.

"Can you give me some warning before you pop in? Whistle or something?"

He whistled the opening bars of the theme from *The Twilight Zone*. "Like that?"

"Not exactly. You got anything a little less…"

"…spooky?" He laughed and did the bird call of the Bob White.

She grinned and opened the fridge to pull out a bottle of lemon-lime soda and finish making her spritzer. "That I can live with." Sipping, she sat sideways on the sofa with her bare feet stretched out.

"Do you always hit the hooch right after work?" he asked.

She took another sip. "Not always. Today was…" She leaned her head back and closed her eyes, "…one of those days."

"I'm glad your car's okay," he said.

"You saw that?"

"Sure."

"What else do you see? Should I wear my bathing suit in the shower?"

"All you have to do is send a mental message that you want privacy. I'm happy to honor that."

"You mean you can read my mind?" She winced. "All the time?"

"There's no judgment, Haley. Things are so different on this side of the veil. Love is all there is. All there is."

She felt a gentle warmth in her heart. It relaxed her as it spread throughout her being.

"How are you, sweetheart? Are you enjoying your life?" For the first time she could remember, he asked questions like he was truly interested. They talked for more than an hour.

Finally, she said, "I'm going to nuke my takeout box from last night. I don't feel like cooking."

"What is it?"

"Cioppino."

"Don't tell me. With mussels and little neck clams?" He moaned. "I miss food so much!" He followed her to the kitchen. When the smell of tomato and basil filled the space, he sighed. "You want to know something really crazy? I can still smell. I can see, hear and smell. I can't taste or feel anything." He drew in a long savoring breath, then said, "Get some rest, honey. Daylon is in his workshop, and I'm going to see what he's up to." His image faded, and he was gone.

Sitting alone at the table, Haley savored her dinner with that warm feeling lingering in her middle. She remembered her dad when they lived in their old house in Oak Park. He had the stocky build of a man who worked with his hands, a quiet man who loved to tinker.

While Haley and Linda were growing up, he would happily spend a Saturday afternoon tuning up his car until it hummed like a sleepy kitten or building a squirrel-proof bird feeder from a pattern in a magazine. He always had a project.

Haley loved to go outside and watch him work. They hardly spoke, but she soaked in his comforting presence. She didn't realize how much she depended on him until he died from colon cancer. He got the diagnosis in July, and he was gone by early September. Haley's youngest child left for college around the same time. That was a cold, empty fall and an even colder winter. She filed for divorce that spring.

Over the next few weeks, life in the new apartment slid into a loose routine. She found a couple of area rugs at a consignment mall along with a brass lamp. When she clicked the living room lamp on, her move in was complete.

One morning, she came outside to see Daylon on a ladder outside her verandah, cleaning out the rain gutters along the edge of the roof. "Morning!" he called as she passed him.

Without looking up, she said, "Good morning." She had a full day ahead, and she was in a hurry. She clicked the unlock button on her key fob. Reaching for the car door, she pulled her hand back like she had received an electric shock.

A furry black body lay in the track where her windshield wipers were.

A dead rat.

Whether she screamed or not, Haley didn't know. For whatever reason, Daylon was down the ladder and beside her before she caught her next breath.

"Who could have done this?" she demanded, as angry as she was shaken. "What kind of twisted…"

"It's a kid's prank," Daylon said. "Immature and senseless."

She stared at him. "A dead animal could mean a lot of things—a warning that I'm next, a threat of worse things to come—a lot of things. He didn't jump up here by himself."

He squinted at her. "Do you have enemies? Disgruntled employees? Information that could put someone in jail?"

"I'm a marriage and family therapist. I know a lot of stuff about a lot of people, but nothing about criminals. I don't have any employees either." She looked away with a grimace. "How awful."

I'm gloves on, eh?

"I've got gloves on. I'll take care of it." He lifted the creature by the tail and headed up the driveway toward the trash bins.

This was an old neighborhood, established in the early 1900s. Although many of the homes were the Arts and Crafts style with a porch topped by a wide gable, this house was the only one of its kind, a Southern style with stacked front porches. The front of the house faced the side of the driveway. The end of the house toward the street had one small window on each level, with a giant fir tree hiding most of it.

The yard was large enough to offer some privacy but small enough to hear dogs barking and party music from the neighbors now and then.

With the rat taken care of, she got into her car, and the engine roared to life. *Whew.* At least it started. She shifted into reverse and stretched to look back.

Two taps on her hood brought her around.

Daylon was at her window, waiting for her to lower it. His hair was cut close on the sides with the top long enough to blow in the breeze. "If you have an idea who might be doing this, I have a private investigator license. I can run background checks," he said. "It costs me forty dollars, so if you can cover that I'll take care of it for you."

"Thanks, Daylon," she said, surprised. "I appreciate that. I'll let you know."

Her heart thumped in her neck. She had a sick feeling in her stomach. For the entire ten-minute drive to work, she concentrated on breathing slowly and deeply to calm herself. Who wanted to scare her? Without a message, the rat couldn't be a warning, could it? She had no enemies that she knew of. Her clients were currently all female, and not one of those women would get within a mile of a dead rat.

30

Who else? An old boyfriend? A client's ex-husband who blamed Haley for a breakup? Well, to be honest, that was possible. She tried to save relationships, but sometimes splitting up was the best option, and she was duty-bound to say so, especially when abuse was involved.

Her phone chirped. At the next red light, she picked it up for a quick peek. Another match from SeniorsMeetup.com. She dropped the phone. No time to look at it now.

Would Eli Loomis do something like this? They hadn't dated long. He had a knack for picking great restaurants, so once or twice a week, they went out and had a nice meal or a movie. He would always fill her in on his problems with his ex and their disagreements on how to raise his seventeen-year-old son. His ex-wife wanted the boy to stay local for college. Eli was more concerned with Ivy League ratings than keeping his child in town—all incredibly fascinating to Haley who had never met the boy or, thankfully, the ex. Haley soon grew tired of him.

One thing about Eli that stuck in Haley's mind was his pinky ring. Hardly anyone wore pinky rings any more. This one was a signet ring made of yellow gold with a flat top engraved with a letter—too worn down to tell which letter.

The car behind her honked. Startled out of her daydreaming, Haley launched her car forward. Parking behind her office, Haley found her notebook inside her shoulder bag. She kept careful notes about her online dates. Actually, she collected information on everyone she met on the site—part of her professional training for staying safe. It was a wacky world out there. She knew that better than most.

Finding Eli's page in the notebook, she scanned the record. She had enough information to do a background check on him.

Turning pages, she looked at two others who were fairly

recent. One had seemed weird from the beginning, but they had some great conversations, so she had agreed to see him again.

The other guy had recently lost his wife. Not a chance that he would do something like this. He was still grieving, although it had been two years since she died. Poor guy. They had been together and in love for forty years.

Of the three, Eli was the youngest at forty-five years old and definitely the most likely to act out.

At their last date, they were at a back table in Rubio's side dining room, when Haley launched into The Breakup Talk. "This has been fun, Eli. You're a wonderful guy, but I think this is our last date."

"What do you mean?" he said, his wide face turning pink, "Have I offended you in some way?"

"It's not that," she said. "You've been great. I just feel like we're in the friend zone." She held out her hand to him. "I've enjoyed spending time with you. Truly, I have."

He stared at her hand for a full second, twisting his lips as though wanting to say something but not sure where to begin. Suddenly, he got to his feet and strode out of the restaurant, leaving her to pay the entire bill. They usually split the cost. Rubio's was the most expensive place in the area.

That's the last she saw of Eli Loomis.

Would he resort to this kind of bizarre behavior to get back at her for breaking off with him? That didn't make sense, but who else could it be?

Chapter Three

Closing the journal with a snap, Haley headed for her office. She had a full load today, seven sessions with a short break for a sandwich while she scribbled notes. She didn't have time to think about Crazy Town right now.

This section of State Street was made up of two long buildings with a small ally between them. On the State Street side, each business had a distinctive front, but the back was a continuous stretch of painted cement blocks. Small signs near the back doors were the only way to determine which business the door belonged to. Alexion was on one side of the alley and A Summer Place bookstore was on the opposite side. Alexion's clients often parked in back.

At a few minutes past five, Haley locked her office door and headed toward the front of the building. She hadn't seen Barb all week. Maybe she was still at her cafe across the street.

To Haley's surprise, she met Barb on the sidewalk near a small red maple tree, its limbs still bare. The calendar said spring had arrived, but local temperatures hadn't read the memo. Bitter winds from Lake Erie continued relentless until May.

Barb was putting something into the trunk of her gleaming red Jaguar. She wore a black leather jacket and black jeans with a heavy gold chain that almost reached her waist. Her glossy dark hair swirled around her shoulders, dancing in the wind.

Barb closed the trunk and told Haley, "I was just coming to find you."

"Ditto," Haley said, smiling. "I thought you might be working tonight."

"Nope. That's what I hire people for." Barb glanced at her watch. "Want to take in a movie? Zoe is on swing shift this week, and I'd rather not go home to an empty house." Zoe, Barb's wife, was a 911 dispatcher who worked odd hours.

Haley smiled. "Now you're talking. I was just going to sit in front of the TV and worry."

"Hop in, *mija*." Barb said, reaching for her car door. "Let's go for a ride!" When the last seatbelt clicked, she shifted into first gear and put the gas pedal down. That Jag loved exercise.

Haley and Barb were both eight years old when they first met. At that time, Barb's family had been in the U.S. for only six months, and Barb was still struggling with English. The girls lived in Orchard Park, a suburb of Buffalo, and their dads worked in the same automobile factory. Barb and Haley went all the way through high school together. They saw each other on vacations while Haley was at the University of Pittsburgh and Barb went to culinary school in New York City.

Their friendship had survived two divorces, four pregnancies, Barb's coming out, plus thousands of other crisis moments and dramas over the past thirty years. Having her office across the street from Barb's café was Haley's dream come true.

Haley leaned back in the Jag's comfortable seat and gratefully stretched her legs. She could already feel the tension unwinding. "What about dinner?" she asked. "Have you eaten?"

"Me? Eat my own food?" She was joking. Barb was tasting food all day long. How she stayed so svelte was a mystery. "How about if we stop in and see Mark and Dori? That okay?"

"Perfect!" Mark and Dori had a small pizza and deli restaurant not far from the theater. They were as much an icon as

like?" She leaned over to get a better look at Haley's phone.

Haley touched the screen. "Let me get into the app." A second later, she gasped.

"Who is it?" Barb demanded.

Haley held out the phone for her to see.

"*Dios mio!*"

Unable to say more, they stared at the smiling face of Linda's gorgeous husband.

Finally, Barb stared into Haley's eyes. "You've got to tell your sister. You've got to."

"Barb. This is the last thing I want to get in the middle of."

"You know they've been having problems for years," Barb went on. "You can't let him get away with this. She needs to know."

Haley groaned. "I'll have to psych myself up for it."

Barb waved her hand in a circle toward Haley's face. "Do your woo-woo thing," she said, and reached for her car ignition. "Find your karmic center...whatever that is...then tell Linda."

The Jaguar roared to life. Haley hung on. When Barb got behind the wheel of that car, she went a little manic. Half an hour later, she dropped Haley off near her vehicle and roared away. After Barb's red Jaguar, Haley's twelve-year-old sedan seemed tame.

When she got home, she flicked on a light and stood in the living room. "Dad?" she called. "Are you there?"

"I'm here," he said from behind her. "What's wrong?"

She told him about finding Scott on the dating site. "This has been going on for as long as they've been married. She catches him. He begs forgiveness. She takes him back. I've lost count the number of times it's happened." She dropped to the sofa in a hopeless gesture. "Now I've got to tell her he's done it again."

Dad sat in the lounge chair. "She'll get through this and be better for it," he said. "She will find herself this time. You'll help her."

"I've tried to help her before, but she won't listen."

"She'll listen this time."

They talked for a few minutes, then Haley excused herself and went to bed. She didn't talk to Linda or Barb until the following Wednesday at the Healing Circle. Things had to percolate in her brain for a while. She needed some kind of plan.

Unpacking a pan of lasagna, Barb gave Haley a pointed look when Linda rushed in. Not that Haley needed a shove in that direction. Giving people tough love is what she did for a living. She just didn't like dishing it out to her friends and family.

Sonia Summers stopped in to say hello. Silver-haired and petite, Sonia was like a tiny, darting bird. Whenever she could, she would pop into the meeting for a few minutes, then leave when someone in the store needed her.

"Sonia!" Barb exclaimed and ran for a quick hug. "Get yourself some lasagna! Tell everyone in the store to come and get some, too."

Sonia laughed with a joy in her voice that made her seem far younger than she was. She picked up three plates, then immediately put them down to dash across the room to hug Cheri over the back of the sofa. When she stood up, Sonia raised one arm toward the ceiling. She gyrated her hips and did a perfect turn. "Naked Yoga tomorrow night! You girls don't know what you're missing."

The room lit up with laughter. Sonia looked like someone's sweet granny, but actually she was one of the girls in those classic skinny-dipping photos from Woodstock.

Haley let the lighthearted mood distract her from the

cannonball in the bottom of her stomach. Dreading the inevitable conversation that was sure to follow, she sat next to Linda on the green sofa. After she had a chance to finish her lunch, Haley leaned close enough to make their conversation private. "Do you have time to come to my place for a few minutes after work today?"

Linda's eyebrows lifted. She focused on Haley. "I'm taking Trevor to a dentist appointment this afternoon."

"How about after dinner?" Haley replied. With Linda's overloaded lifestyle, waiting for a better time would never happen.

Linda's eyes narrowed until a crease formed between her eyebrows. "Now you're scaring me. I'll be there around seven. I'll text you."

Haley picked up a roasted chicken from the grocery store on her way home from work. She was making a thick sandwich on sourdough when her dad whistled his Bob White call. A moment later, he was sitting at her dining room table.

"Linda's coming over," Haley said, opening the fridge door to put away the mustard. "I'm going to spill the beans on Scott."

He flexed his muscular hand. "I wish I could take a swipe at him," he said. "She doesn't deserve this."

"It's about time she found that out," Haley retorted. "If I'm this tired of his shenanigans, you know she has to be tired of him even more."

Linda knocked on the door at a few minutes past seven. Dad went to a corner of the living room as Haley opened the door to let in a gust of freezing wind along with her pink-faced sister.

As soon as the door closed, Linda said, "What is it?"

Haley held out her phone.

A caught breath and Linda closed her eyes with an exhale

that lasted so long it seemed to leave her smaller with tired lines deepening on her face.

"I'm so sorry," Haley said, touching the sleeve of her padded jacket. "Sit down for a moment." She gently urged her toward the sofa where she sat and leaned back, eyes still closed.

"Can I get you some water?" Haley asked.

"I knew it would happen," she said, slowly shaking her head. "I knew it..."

"There's no way to prepare yourself for something like this," Haley said, pouring a glass of water from the fridge. When Linda ignored the glass, Haley set it on the coffee table.

Linda pressed her forehead. "I need a moment..."

"Take your time. I'm going to my room." Giving her father a meaningful look, she headed down the hall and quietly closed the door behind her.

When she turned around, Dad was less than a foot in front of her.

She gasped. "Can you give me a little space?"

"Sorry." He backed away. "I'm going home with her, Haley. I won't be around for a while. I just wanted you to know."

"I thought you had to stay in range of the power station."

"Yes, to materialize I do. I can also hitch a ride with someone I love and who loves me back. I can project a sense of comfort to Linda while I'm with her. If you need me, call out to me, and I'll come back."

Haley nodded. "I wish I could hug you right now, Dad. I really miss your hugs." Tears sprang to her eyes.

Suddenly, she felt the same warmth in her heart as it spread throughout her being. The loving look in his eyes had her crying in earnest. "I love you, Dad. I'm so glad you're here."

"I love you, too, sweetheart. Just call out, and I'll be here in a tiny New York second." He faded away and was gone.

Haley went to the bathroom sink to splash her face. When she returned to the living room, Linda was staring at a black-and-white framed print on the wall. No sign of tears.

Haley sat down near her. "What are you going to do?"

"I'm going home." She lifted her cell phone from her lap. "Tomorrow at four o'clock I have an appointment with my attorney." She picked up the water glass and took a long drink. "Thank you, Haley."

"I'm here whenever you need me."

Linda nodded, as though from far away. She got to her feet and went out.

Haley stepped outside and waited while Linda backed out of the driveway. The frigid wind washed over Haley's face, and she drew in a deep, cold breath. In her counselling practice, she had learned to release her emotions after listening to someone else's troubles—the same way a doctor washes her hands after seeing a patient. But family was different.

For a few seconds, she allowed herself to imagine Scott in a series of painful predicaments, then she took a deep breath of cold, cleansing air and let it go.

The next evening after work, Haley carefully went through the notepad from her purse and organized the information on the three men she had recently dated. Tucking rewritten pages into her purse, she had a long, hot shower and went to bed.

The next morning, Haley paused on her way to work to knock on Daylon's door.

He opened it wearing a blue flannel shirt, jeans and white socks—big surprise. Holding a cup of coffee, he said, "Come in. It's too cold to stand outside."

She had never been inside his place before. Stepping across

the threshold, she said, "I'm glad for a coat with a hood, that's for sure." She pulled the hood back and glanced around. His place was exactly like hers—a center hall with a living room-kitchen combination on the left and bedroom door on the right. Her apartment had light gray laminate flooring, but his floor covering was a brown pebble-patterned vinyl, showing wear in the doorways and in front of the sink.

A brown leather sofa sat under the big front window, the same position as her own. That sofa filled most of the living room with a matching lounge chair on the side, facing a big-screen TV attached to the wall. She had never liked leather furniture. It was too hard and cold.

"Coffee?" he asked.

"No, thanks. I have an early appointment, and I need to keep moving." She reached into the side pocket of her bag. "I made a list of the men I've dated recently with their details." She handed the page to him. "I'd like to take you up on your offer for background checks."

He glanced at the list and then at her. "How did you get all this information on them?"

She grinned. "I'm a counselor. I listen."

"...and take notes," he said, raising his eyebrows as he scanned the paper. "I'll let you know when I have something to tell."

"Thanks." With a quick good-bye, she headed for her car. It started on the first try.

When she arrived home that afternoon, Daylon's door opened. "I've got something for you," he called out. "Want to see it?"

"I'd like to change out of these clothes first," she said. "I'll be down in a few minutes."

The moment she stepped through her door, she kicked off her shoes. She headed to the fridge to pour lemon-lime soda over ice and add a tiny splash of Riesling. She took her time sliding into her comfy jeans and soft gray sweatshirt.

Her bed looked so inviting. Daylon could wait ten more minutes while she stretched out on her comforter. Her bedroom took its color scheme from the amethyst crystal tower on her dresser. It had center stage on a wide strip of velvet in eggplant color with her earrings lined in symmetrical rows beside it. She loved the way the dark color made her earrings pop under the light. The only jewelry she wore was earrings. Bracelets, necklaces and rings bothered her. Every time she tried wearing them, she soon pulled them off.

She cued up the short version of her meditation music on her phone, scootched around on the bed to get comfortable and closed her eyes.

Half an hour later, she came awake. Laughing softly as though at a private joke, she rubbed her face to try to look less sleepy and dragged a wide-tooth comb through her blond hair, a lost cause with the wind these days. She pulled on short mukluks and found her padded jacket.

When Daylon opened the door, she gave him a guilty grin.

He grinned back. "Something happen?"

Pulling off her hood, she shook her head. "I stretched out for one minute and fell asleep. You still want to do this now? Do you have plans for tonight?"

He waved for her to come inside. "My only plans are to show you what I found. Which isn't much, I'm afraid." His small dining room table held a laptop and several Chinese food cartons. "This delivery just got here. Are you hungry? Plates are in the cabinet by the sink."

The food smelled delightful. She helped herself to shrimp fried rice and an egg roll. Daylon pulled a wooden chair closer to him, so she could sit down and see the laptop.

"I got a hit on one of them…" His voice trailed off as he peered at the screen, reading. "Eli Loomis." He picked up a food carton, twirled chopsticks around and lifted a bundle of noodles to his mouth.

She sat down. "Really? I just broke up with him. He could be the guy." She frowned. "Although...he didn't act like a stalker."

Daylon glanced at her. Still chewing, he said, "You're the expert. What does a stalker act like exactly?"

"You know, neediness, pent-up anger, revengeful…" She broke off, considering. Finally, she admitted, "Eli did have some of those traits."

He gazed at the screen. "See this? Loomis had a restraining order about eight years ago."

"Oh, I know about that." Haley scanned the document. "His ex-wife kicked him out of the house and wouldn't let him back in to pick up his stuff. She called the law on him."

"Any confirmation about that story? Are you sure it's the truth?"

She hesitated. "Not really. I've never met his ex or any of his friends."

"Is it possible this guy goes haywire when he feels rejected?"

She sighed. "After all I've seen in my practice, anything is possible. What can I do, Daylon? How can I stop him?"

"You already have motion-activated lights. Security cameras would be the next step."

She winced. "That sounds expensive. Maybe he got the angst out of his system. Maybe he won't come back."

"Your car is obviously an easy target. Living on the second floor is a big advantage. You probably won't have any problems up there. Besides, I would hear if anyone goes up those stairs."

Her lips formed a little grin in spite of herself. "So, are you a German Shepherd or a dachshund or a...?"

He chuckled and handed her another egg roll.

After spending a hundred and twenty dollars on background checks plus the cost of the diagnostic on her car, Haley was a bit reluctant to rush out and add more stress to her already stretched budget. Not that she was in poverty, but she was careful with spending and hated to dig into her savings. She decided to wait a while before buying camera equipment. Tired of thinking about it, she pushed everything out of her mind and spent the weekend reading and recharging.

When Tuesday arrived with no incidents, she told herself all the stalking nonsense was over. That evening after dinner, she curled up with a cup of tea and a book. A few minutes past eight, her phone chirped, a text. "Hey, want to get coffee and talk?" It was from Eli Loomis.

Her heart lurched. What should she do?

Get a grip, Haley. What would you usually do? Nothing.

She dropped the phone to the sofa beside her. After a breakup she always went a hundred percent no contact. This time, though, she felt a twinge of fear. When he didn't get an answer, that might set him off again. She took a breath. All she could do was wait and see.

She didn't sleep well that night or the next. Nothing happened, not even another text.

The next morning, Haley arrived at the office with a feeling of relief. This was where she got out of her head and into the zone.

45

Her office was barely large enough for a small sofa and club chair for clients, a wingback chair on the side for Haley along with a low coffee table that held only a box of tissues. Shoved into a corner of the room, her desk had a swiveling chair, so she could turn around and face a client from the there. Except for a soft pink faux-fur throw flung across an arm of the sofa, everything was in shades of white, silver and gray, even the artwork on the walls.

Wednesday was Healing Circle day. She tried to keep her eleven o' clock appointment on time and end at fifty minutes. Today, however, they went all the way to noon. When the client left, Haley saw a folded note someone had slipped under the door. *See you at the Healing Circle. We went early.*

Cheri & Frankie

Frankie Joseph was a former social worker, now life coach, tarot reader and energy healer. She was a couple of years shy of thirty and close friends with Cheri. They acted like sisters, although they were more than forty years apart in age.

Cheri was red-haired and freckled, of Irish descent, and Frankie had come to the U.S. from St. Lucia as a teenager. Somehow, they still managed a strong resemblance, partly due to Frankie's passion for what she called "woo-woo fashion." Most of Cheri's clothes were a one-of-a-kind upcycled style, beautifully handcrafted by Frankie.

Barb had to cater a wedding today, so the meeting would have no buffet line. On her way out, Haley stopped by the office kitchen to pick up a container of Greek yogurt from the fridge.

The moment Haley strolled into the meeting, the chatter went silent, all eyes on her. "What?" she said. When no one replied, her heart rate picked up.

"Sit down," Cheri said, touching the open space next to her.

"Flo has an appointment this afternoon," Haley said, tears flowing. She sniffed. "I've never lost a client to domestic violence before. So awful. She was just getting her life back."

Frankie came back to the group. Tall and willowy like Cheri, Frankie had hundreds of tiny braids reaching halfway down her back, with the left side of her head shaved close.

"I have a number," Frankie said. Although she had been in the U.S. almost fifteen years, her Caribbean accent was mostly unchanged. "She is in the temporary group home. They won't release her until they clear her father," which came out more like *fadah*.

Haley said, "Her father is a suspect?"

Cheri moved over, so Frankie could sit next to Haley.

"I'm texting you the number," Frankie said. "You can call them and try to get permission to see the child."

Haley sipped tea and breathed in the steam. "I'll have to reschedule my afternoon appointments. Not that I could do them anyway." She huffed out a big breath, leaned far back and rubbed the center of her forehead with her free hand.

"If you're heading directly to the group home, I'll drive you," Cheri announced. Her voice expanded to include the group. "We're all upset, so let's go into our breathwork now, okay?"

Closing her eyes, Haley carefully held her mug in her lap and let the meditation take her away.

A few minutes later, the Healing Circle broke up early. Haley called Fleeta's case worker and learned that no one could visit the girl until she had been fully debriefed by investigators, probably late that afternoon. Haley would get a call when Fleeta was cleared for a visit.

Instead of going back to her office, Haley sat a few moments longer to text her afternoon clients, then went home.

Daylon's blue pickup truck arrived at the house just ahead of her. He stood in the driveway, waiting for her to step out of her car. "Everything okay?" he asked.

Without mentioning names, she told him what happened. "I'm afraid this is domestic violence. She just broke up with her boyfriend."

"Did he also have a grudge against you?"

She nodded. "I wondered if he would end up suing me. It wouldn't be the first time." She took a step toward the house, and he joined her.

"People take you to court?"

"Oh, yeah. When a client has an abuser, sometimes that person will go after the counselor for interfering in the relationship. In six years of practice, I've been sued three times. The last time was two months ago. I had wondered if Pauly might be number four."

Daylon's eyebrows drew down. "He could be your stalker, you know."

Haley gasped. "He would do it, too." She pressed her forehead. "I have to go in and rest. This has me pretty shook up."

He nodded and stepped away. As she headed upstairs, he called after her. "Let's catch up later."

Haley dropped her purse on the coffee table and kicked off her shoes. She made herself a wine spritzer. Sitting sideways on the couch, she stretched out her legs and pulled the throw around her. Grief washed over her in waves.

She let herself cry it out. After a while, she lay her head on the soft arm of the couch and drifted into light sleep.

Her business phone buzzed twice before she scooped it up.

Fleeta could see her now.

Splashing her face with cold water, she did a little makeup

repair and headed out. The group home was across town, about six miles away in an old neighborhood.

As Haley parked in the gravel driveway, the street lights came on. The house looked historic with two fluted columns holding up a small portico shading the front door.

Before she knocked, a young woman wearing a light blue uniform blouse and dark blue pants opened the door. She wore a police badge and a gun. Behind her, two box fluorescent lights gleamed in the ceiling, one of them with a flickering tube.

"I need to see some ID," the policewoman said. She carefully looked at Haley's credentials, produced a clipboard for signing in, then led Haley down the hall. The place smelled like hospital antiseptic.

Fleeta had a small private room with a single bed, a chest of drawers and no nightstand. Haley walked in to see Fleeta curled on top of the white bedspread. Instantly, the girl bolted into Haley's arms and held tight, her face buried in Haley's neck.

Haley held her for a moment.

When they sat on the side of the bed, Fleeta sobbed, "Mom...Mom!"

"I know, sweetheart." Haley wiped her own tears with the back of her hand. "You're in this place to keep you safe, not because you've done anything wrong. You understand that, right?"

Fleeta nodded. She was so young to have seen such grief and loss. When other girls her age were giggling over boys and practicing piano, she had to work through her twin brother's disease and death, her parents' divorce... and now this.

Haley's maternal instinct kicked in. She fought off the desire to take Fleeta home with her. She sat with Fleeta for about thirty minutes, not talking much. What Fleeta needed right now was a

51

comforting presence, not words.

After a while, Haley said, "Rest as much as you can over the weekend. I will come back to see you on Monday."

"I want to go to my dad," Fleeta said, pleading. She had the same piercing blue eyes and black hair as her mother.

"I know. But for right now, you need to stay here until the police can find the person who did this. Have you heard from your dad?"

She shook her head.

"I'm sure he has tried to call you. They won't let anyone talk to you until things get sorted out. The only reason I got in is because I'm your counselor." She reached for her purse. "Can I bring you a book? Something else?"

"They have books here, but I can't read. I can't even watch a movie." A tear ran down her cheek. "I want to go to my dad."

"How about a treat? Ice cream?"

Fleeta lay back on her bed. Her eyes drifted closed, as though too tired to go on talking. The wall above her head had a smudge of sticker residue. "Fries and a milkshake," she murmured.

"Oh, heathy stuff," Haley said, with a gentle smile. "Vanilla? Chocolate?"

"Vanilla." She drew in a shaky breath.

"Would you like me to call your dad for you? I can give him a message."

She nodded. "Tell him I want to be with him."

Haley pulled the bedspread up from the side to cover the girl. Fleeta rolled over to face the wall, taking the spread with her. She seemed asleep already.

Haley said good-bye and promised to come back on Monday. She waited until she reached home before she called Fleeta's father. This was her first time to speak with him. She had no idea what to expect.

As soon as she identified herself, Mr. Yeager bellowed into her ear, "Where is my daughter? I've been trying to find her all day!" He had the brittle edge of panic in his voice.

"She's in protective custody. She asked that I call you and let you know she's all right. Please cooperate with the police and give them your alibi, Mr. Yeager. The sooner this is cleared up, the sooner they'll let you take Fleeta home with you."

"Am I a suspect?" he yelled. "This is a nightmare! I was nowhere near Flo's place."

"Mr. Yeager, I have nothing to do with the police. I'm here to help your daughter. She's had a rough time, as I'm sure you can imagine."

He paused, then went on more quietly. "I'm sorry. I've been worried out of my mind. Please, tell her I'll come and get her as soon as I can."

Haley gave him her business cell number in case of emergency, then got off the phone as quickly as she could. Her head hurt, and she was exhausted beyond belief. She hadn't eaten dinner, and she had no energy for her usual shower. She turned off the lights and went to bed.

Monday was her day off, but Haley spent all morning at police headquarters answering questions. Her request to visit Fleeta had put Haley on their radar, so they called her to request her presence. She told the two detectives what she could about Flo's messy divorce, about Pauly and the recent breakup, about Flo's mental state the last time they met, ending by emphasizing the fact that she couldn't turn over her notes without a subpoena.

"What about known associates?" the bald one named Banks asked. "She turned off her security system near the time of her death, so we're looking at people she knew. Do you know her friends, family? Even if they weren't in the area, they might know something about Flo's life that would help us."

Haley considered. "I'm not sure of names. We always talked in terms of her sister or her mother without identifying who they are."

Banks handed her his card. "We have Pauly Hammond in custody as a material witness. We can only hold him for forty-eight hours, so if you think of any details about him that slipped your mind today, please be sure to email or text me immediately."

She nodded and dropped the card into her purse. "Detective, can I ask you something?"

He waited for her to go on.

"If someone has a stalker, what kind of evidence would you need to arrest him...or her?"

"Unless you have clear video evidence, you're going to have a hard time prosecuting," he said. "Unfortunately, people who engage in that behavior usually know about video surveillance. They typically cover up with hoodies, sunglasses..."

"...masks," his young, blond partner chimed in.

Ignoring him, Banks went on. "Law enforcement can only take action after a crime has been committed. You'll have to be proactive to protect yourself. Be prepared to gather evidence for an arrest. You need video evidence, so get video cameras installed, that kind of thing."

Haley had pretty much expected that answer, but she still didn't like hearing it.

On the way to her car, her intuition became a loud alarm, telling her she should have video cameras installed right away. That brought up a whole list of things to do—permission from Sonia and Martin, buying the right equipment and finding an installer—just for starters. She didn't want to deal with all that right now. Not only did all this cost money, it also used up her time.

When she left police headquarters, Haley headed toward the group home to visit Fleeta. She made a quick detour to grab a sandwich for a late lunch and arrived a little after two o'clock.

The sunshine felt good, so Haley and Fleeta found a seat at a picnic table in the backyard. The grassy lawn had a chain link fence with a prickly hedge surrounding it. Haley had brought the promised fries and vanilla milkshake.

After some chit chat while Fleeta ate, Haley said, "Are you having dreams?"

Fleeta nodded. She was so pale her skin looked translucent. Blue veins showed at her temples and the backs of her hands. Her eyes looked bruised from crying. "Sometimes I wake up yelling, and the night nurse has to come into my room. She lets me sleep with the closet light on."

"That happens a lot after someone has a shock. Those will fade after a while."

Fleeta drew in a long breath. "When we got back from visiting my uncle, Mom dropped me off for a slumber party. She was supposed to pick me up the next afternoon, but she didn't come. I couldn't get Mom on the phone, so my friend Jennifer's mom dropped me off. I have a key, so that was fine." She paused. "Something was weird because Mom's car was in the garage. I could see it through the window on my way to the door."

Haley wished she could have a few choice words with Jennifer's mom for letting Fleeta go inside alone. She waited for Fleeta to go on.

Fleeta winced and turned her face away. "She was lying on the floor in the kitchen. I didn't see any blood or anything. She looked like she was sleeping, but I couldn't wake her up." Her face twisted. "Was it Pauly? I hate him. He's such a loser! He used to yell at Mom for seeing you every week. He wanted her to stop going."

Haley said, "I know. But what if it wasn't Pauly? Maybe someone was robbing the house when she got home, and she walked in on them. The house was empty for two whole weeks."

"The police asked me that, but nothing was taken. Everything was still there." She shivered. "I want to go to my dad."

"That's the next step when they are sure you are safe."

They talked a few minutes longer, then Haley said good-bye. Before leaving, she promised to come back later in the week.

Haley drove two blocks and pulled into a parking space to make notes while Fleeta's story was fresh in her mind. Whoever hurt Flo was no stranger to that house. More than ever, Pauly fit the bill. She dropped her notebook into her purse. Was Pauly also after her?

Chapter Five

Haley walked into that week's Healing Circle to see Barb ladling Italian wedding soup into crockery she had brought with her. Each bowl had a piece of crusty garlic bread on the side. Barb wore her white chef's coat with her dark hair pulled high into its typical messy twist.

When she spotted Haley, Barb dropped what she was doing to meet her at the door. "Hey, are you okay? I had a wedding, so I haven't been able to call." She took inventory of Haley's appearance. "You look tired."

Haley stepped to the side, so they weren't blocking the door. "Stressed is more like it. Not only did I lose my weekend, but I spent it…" She shook her head and huffed out a breath.

Barb got it. "You want to come to my place tonight for Chinese takeout and a chick flick?" Barb had an ironclad rule: she didn't cook outside her business. Zoe was a wonderful cook. If Zoe didn't feel like cooking, they went out or called for delivery.

"Let me see how the day goes," Haley said. "If I'm not totally wiped after my last client, I'll take you up on that. I need a distraction, for sure."

Sonia stepped up, and Haley paused to hug her. Barb drifted back to the food.

"Sonia, I need to ask you something," Haley said. She told her about the video cameras.

Frowning with concern, Sonia said, "This really has been a

tough week for you, hasn't it? I had no idea you were having problems. A stalker, too? Incredible." She glanced toward the seating area. People were quieting down for the meeting. She whispered, "Do whatever you need to do. Just stay safe. Daylon might be able to help you."

Haley and Sonia picked up their soup bowls and found seats. Linda hurried into the room, and Barb got up to help her with the food.

Everyone in the Healing Circle shared their announcements on local events and reminders. When that part of the conversation died, Cheri said, "Haley, now that you've had time to finish your lunch, do you know any more about what happened to Flo Yeager?"

"Not much except for what's been in the papers. The police do suspect foul play, but they are still piecing together what happened."

Linda said, "Did you know her, Haley?" For someone who had recently had her marriage disintegrate, Linda looked rested, a few years younger, actually.

Haley nodded. "I can't say more, but yes I knew her."

Barb spoke up. "She lives down the street from me. Did you know that?"

Haley said, "I forgot about that. You must have had some excitement around there for a few days. Did anyone in the neighborhood see anything?"

Barb shook her head. "Zoe had some cops knock on the door, but she was out during the timeframe they mentioned. She didn't see anything. As for me, I've hardly been home this week." She paused, frowning. "My back door neighbor stopped me this morning as I was leaving for work. She said that someone saw a man running out of Flo's house that afternoon."

"Who was it?" Haley asked.

Barb shrugged. "That came through the grapevine, so it's not reliable. I don't have details anyway." She hesitated. "I do remember one thing, though. It's not about that day, but I do know that her ex-husband was really creepy."

"You know him?" Haley asked.

"Everyone on that cul-de-sac knows him. He used to drive by Flo's house at least once a week, going slow and staring. He's got a screw loose." She shivered.

Haley sat back. Flo did mention that her ex was always hanging around. She had never mentioned feeling threatened, like he might harm her.

"When's the last time you saw him?" Haley asked.

Barb tilted her head, thinking. "I can't remember. Let me text Zoe." She reached for her phone.

Cheri moved the group into the meditation, and the meeting ended a few minutes before one. Cheri and Frankie walked with Haley back to the office.

Cheri said, "Any more stalking incidents?"

Haley shook her head. "I'm hoping for the best. In the meantime, I'm installing more security equipment." She sighed. "This time slot would be Flo's weekly appointment. I haven't filled it yet."

"Switch someone around," Cheri said. "You don't need that sinking feeling. You have enough on your mind."

Haley updated notes and filed insurance paperwork until quarter to two. Val Jansen came in every Wednesday at two p.m. She and her husband Jovan had first come to her for couple's therapy at the suggestion of their pastor. Val was the daughter of a local farm family. Jovan was as tall and muscular as a Viking. After five years of trying, they hadn't been able to conceive a child. The stress had created quite a bit of strain between them.

The Jansen's lived on an almost-off-grid homestead a mile outside of town. One of the larger farmers in the area let them have two acres and a house in exchange for Jovan's help during planting and harvest. When he wasn't working off their rent, he grew a garden and kept chickens and pigs. For cash, they sold vegetables and eggs. Val also earned an income as a regional distributor for a multi-level marketing company.

From their first visit, Haley saw red flags in their relationship. Jovan came to the sessions to please their pastor, but he wouldn't participate. When he did speak, he blamed his wife and took no personal responsibility for his own behavior and attitudes. As long as Jovan was in the room, Val zipped up. With neither of them talking, Haley was on the verge of ending their sessions altogether.

The moment Haley had Jovan leave the room, Val relaxed and seemed like a different person: intelligent, articulate and genuinely lovely.

One day, Val arrived for their appointment alone with bruises on her wrists and her cheek. She said Jovan had pinned her against the living room wall and hit her across the face because she had come home from a network meeting half an hour later than he had expected.

Haley advised her to file a police report for domestic violence. When she did, a storm of events followed. Val returned home to live with her parents. Jovan soon discovered he couldn't manage the farm alone. He sued Haley for malpractice, but the case didn't get to court because the judge threw it out.

Over the following months, Val's cheerful, outgoing personality became more and more evident. Her business grew, and she won a car in a sales contest. Jovan disappeared from

Haley's awareness. Aside from reports from Val, Haley had no idea what Jovan was doing or where he was.

At two, Val arrived in a flurry of energy. "Guess what happened," she said before she took her coat off. "I'm flying to California next week for a conference." She squeezed her arms to her sides, hugging herself. "I can't wait."

"Good for you," Haley said, smiling. "Tell me all about it." What a breath of fresh air this woman was.

Val launched into her story about opening a major market in a neighboring town through the contacts of one of her customers. Haley listened attentively, but in the back of her mind she felt a tiny tap-tap-tapping, like an angel calling to her, telling her to visit Flo's house. Some people called it a Spidey sense. She called it her intuition.

By the time the day ended, the feeling had become more like a clanging bell at a railroad crossing. Haley got into her car and knew she was headed to Flo's house. She couldn't say why. She just had to go there.

Before she set off, she shivered and turned up the car's heater. Was Flo trying to tell her something? Even before her dad showed up in her living room, Haley had been receiving messages from the other side for years. No one had ever appeared to her before.

Closing her eyes and breathing to calm herself, Haley paused to check in. All she got was an even stronger urge to head over there. She backed out of the parking space and put the car in drive.

This was a familiar route since Barb lived on the same street as Flo. Englewood township encompassed roughly a five-mile radius from the downtown area. Half the population lived within the town's boundaries. This was Pennsylvania countryside at its best—rolling hills, streams and lots of trees crisscrossed by narrow winding roads without paved shoulders. Even near big cities, the roadways felt like the country.

Turning onto Barb's street, Haley took a slow turn in the cul-de-sac past Flo's house. A two-story home with white vinyl siding, it had a gray roof and black shutters. A matching detached garage connected to the house by a covered sidewalk. Yellow police tape made an X over the front door.

Suddenly, a small riding mower roared into the front yard. It moved so fast that Haley worried about the safety of the driver. She hit the brake, so she could watch him. Why was he mowing in early May? Then she saw a small green container behind the mower. He was spreading something over the lawn, like fertilizer or something.

One more glance at the driver, and she pulled away. He hunkered over the steering wheel, bundled in a thick coat and a cap with earflaps. He looked chunky, but that could be all the layers he had on.

When Haley rounded the circle on her way out, Barb's Jaguar pulled into her driveway. Haley parked nearby and got out. Wearing a short wool jacket over her chef's coat, Barb came toward her, a puzzled look on her face.

Haley said, "Hey, I had an impulse to see Flo's house. Who is that on the riding lawn mower?"

Barb turned to check. "It's Joey Everly, her next-door neighbor. He takes care of her yard work. Has for years. He's a friendly guy. Everyone loves Joey."

"Tell me about him." The mower went behind the house and took the noise with it.

"Uhmmm… From what I know—which is mostly from the neighborhood—he took care of his mother until she passed a few years ago...never married... lives alone.... He's handy. Whenever something breaks, like the weed eater, Zoe takes it over to him, and he brings it back fixed in a couple of days." She shivered. "Want to come inside? I'm freezing." Her phone pinged. "Oh, that's the restaurant. I've gotta go."

"Thanks, Barb," Haley said. "I can't stay. Too much to do. See you later." She hurried back to her still-running car, and Barb jogged up the driveway.

Closing the car door, Haley reached for her pen and notebook to record what she had learned about the lawn guy. Looking over her notes, she again wondered if her stalker and Flo's murderer were the same person. If so, he had already killed once. The possibility terrified her.

When she arrived home, she knocked on Daylon's door. No answer. Strange, his truck was here. She knocked again. Still no answer. Finally, she headed upstairs. As she came around the corner of her verandah, she spotted him in the backyard with a spade, digging in the grass.

She went into her apartment long enough to set down her purse and change her shoes, then went out to speak with him. The forsythia bush on the edge of the lawn was still yellow, although showing signs of wear. Next to it, pink buds covered a row of peony bushes.

He looked up when she reached the edge of the plot—a small rectangle of bare earth in an expanse of lawn.

"What is this for?" she asked. "Flowers or vegetables?"

He stood, the flat spade propped under his hands. "A vegetable garden just big enough for two of each for pollination. I've got tomatoes, zucchini, green peppers... You get the picture." He lifted a shovel filled with dirt and turned it over. "This is too small for a rototiller, and I need the exercise."

"Don't let me hold you up," she said. "I can talk while you do that." He went back to turning over the earth. "I had a talk with the police. They tell me I need video footage in order to prosecute a stalker."

He stopped working and peered at her, his hand outstretched. "OK, hold on a second. You had a talk with the police?"

She told him about Flo. "I had to give a statement, so I took the opportunity to get some information. Long story short, I have to get video cameras installed."

He bent over to break up a big chunk of clay. Glancing at her, he said, "You have a lot of options, Haley. One of them is to get a home security company to come in and take care of everything for you."

She sighed. "In the first place, that will take time, and I'd rather have them put in right away. In the second place, that will raise my monthly expenses quite a bit. I'd rather not go that route if I don't have to."

He nodded. "OK, you can get outdoor video cameras that hook into a web application. They record directly to the cloud, so even if someone destroys the camera, the footage is safe. With those, you can also see what the camera sees via a cellphone app. If someone knocks on your door, you could pull up the app and check out who they are before you open."

"That sounds like the best option."

He nodded. "When I finish here, I'll text you some links for cameras, and we can go from there. I can pick them up locally and have them in for you by tomorrow or the next day." He stopped digging to look at her. "How's that?"

"Thank you, Daylon."

He went back to digging, and she went inside to heat up leftover chicken casserole for dinner.

Her personal phone chirped as she dried her dinner plate. After a couple of texts with Daylon, she put down the phone. At least the cameras were off her mind.

The next afternoon, as Haley parked her car, Daylon came around the corner of the house. He headed straight for her, a worried look on his face. "I have something I want to tell you."

She lost her breath for a second. "What is it?"

"I was at the automotive parts store this afternoon. You know the one on Maple Ave?"

She nodded.

"A short, tubby guy was in there shooting off his mouth to the men who work behind the counter. He was talking about his girlfriend's therapist and how it's her fault that his girlfriend is now dead."

Haley went dizzy for a second. "What?"

"Yeah. He was blaming this therapist loud and long."

"Did he use any names?"

"I got some of it on a recording. I didn't get his face on the video, but I did pick up his voice." He pulled out his cell phone and found the video for her.

The image showed light gray tile and a rack of windshield wipers. A raspy shrill voice said, "She should be arrested. I'm telling you, she got my girl killed."

A deep voice called out, "What do you need, Daylon?" and the video ended there.

Haley went weak. "That was Pauly. I'd know his voice anywhere." She pressed both hands against her cheeks. "When he got out of police custody, I had another incident." She shivered. "I'm scared, Daylon. I'm afraid he'll come after me next."

"Put me on speed dial. No matter where you are, if you have

any trouble, I'm the second call after 911, okay? We're gonna to get this whack job." He tapped the hood of her car twice for emphasis and headed toward the back yard.

The following morning at the office, Haley decided to get a second cup of coffee. She hadn't slept well the night before. When she stepped into the hallway, she glanced at the big window facing the sidewalk. The same guy from Flo's yard was standing across the street next to a big planter filled with red tulips. He had on the same brown bomber jacket and matching hat with earflaps.

Forgetting her coffee, she brushed past Frankie, who was in the waiting room talking to the receptionist. Haley planted herself in front of the plate glass window and demanded, "Who is that?"

Frankie came to stand beside her to get a better view. She had on a jean jacket with white lace wings appliqued to the back. "That's Joey Everly," she said.

Haley turned to her. "You know him?"

"A little." Frankie paused, curious. "Why? What is going on?"

Haley took a breath. "I saw him somewhere, and I want to know more about him."

Interested, Frankie held on. "This is about your stalker?"

Haley shook her head. "He's Flo's neighbor."

"Yesterday, he was at the cafe while I was there," Frankie said, her chin lifting as she remembered. "He was talking really loud. He said he saw someone running across Flo's back yard that afternoon. He kept going on about it."

Haley said, "Yesterday, something weird happened. After work, I got a strong intuition to drive by Flo's place, and he was there on a riding mower."

"Maybe Cheri should do a reading," Frankie said. "Flo might

66

have a message for you. Cheri can help you figure it out."

"Usually, I pick up messages myself," Haley replied. "For some reason, not this time."

Frankie nodded. "Unfortunately, you cannot pick up the phone and call the other side."

Haley's phone chirped, and she laughed. "Maybe that's the message I've been waiting for." The text said she could pick up her Martha Washington cabinet that afternoon. Finally, after two months it was ready.

She touched Frankie's arm. "Thanks, hon."

"No problem." She returned to her conversation with Brenda at the receptionist's desk.

That afternoon, Haley picked up the table before she went home. It looked better than it had for years. They had even polished the brass marker that said: Cowan: The Original Martha Washington Sewing Cabinet.

When she got home, Daylon's truck was gone. She left the table in the trunk, thinking she would ask Daylon to help her when he got home. She was taking no more chances. Besides, she wanted to talk to him about the video equipment, anyway.

As it grew dark, she looked through the miniblinds covering her front window. He still wasn't back. A little worried, she spoke into her phone to text him, "Hi Daylon." The message came out: *Hi Dylan.* Irritated, she erased it and typed instead: Just checking in on the cameras.

Daylon replied: My son Scott was in a serious car accident. He's been in surgery for three hours so far.

Haley: So sorry to hear that! I hope he's okay.

Daylon: It's his leg. They say he's going to be fine after some rehab. Rough day for all of us. I have your cameras in the truck. Tomorrow, I'll put them up for you.

Haley: No hurry at all. So sorry about your son.

The next morning, misty rain and fog made the air seem heavy. The steps felt a little slick, so she took extra care. Daylon's parking spot was still empty. Poor guy. She would call him later.

Newly blooming Stella de Oro daylilies filled the verge between the porch and the sidewalk like yellow beams of light on a dismal day.

When she reached the sidewalk, she gasped. On the pavement behind her car, the Martha Washington cabinet lay smashed like someone had beat it against the macadam. She ran to her car and saw the glove compartment open and empty. Her CDs were gone, her cup holder, every scrap of paper and every pen. Her jacket was missing from the back seat. The trunk was also empty—no jack, no spare, no emergency kit she always kept there. The entire car was stripped clean.

Furious, terrified, devastated at the loss of her precious cabinet—she dialed 911.

Chapter Six

Shaking so much she could hardly type, Haley texted her first two clients of the day to reschedule. She might have to stay here a while.

She bent closer to look at the damage to her grandmother's table. It was an irreplaceable family heirloom. Hot tears burned her eyes. Some things are just gone forever. No amount of saying *Sorry* would take away these feelings of betrayal and loss. This was one of those moments.

Nothing in the car had any significant resale value for anyone else. *Why do this?*

Waiting for the police to arrive, she didn't touch anything. Shivering from nerves and cold, she had to get out of the misty rain, so she decided to go back into her apartment and watch from the window.

Fifteen minutes later, a patrol car pulled in and a massive man got out. He had on a black jacket with so much equipment around his waist, he held his arms out from his body as he walked. With a stony expression, he glanced over the damaged table and the open trunk of the car.

Pulling up the hood of her coat, Haley hurried down the steps.

The officer introduced himself as Sgt. Kirk. His voice sounded heavy and flat. "What happened here?" he said, his dark eyes boring into Haley.

Why did she suddenly feel guilty? "When I came out to go

to work, this is what I found. That's all I know."

He looked at the house, scanning the roofline and the porches. "I don't see any cameras," he said, as though accusing her.

"I'm having some installed today."

"So, you've had trouble before now?" He pulled out a cell phone and took pictures. "Can I see some ID?"

Haley handed him her driver's license. He took pictures of both sides of the license while she told him about the two previous incidents.

"Do you have any idea who might have done this?"

"Nothing definite." She told him about her counseling practice. "It might be a disgruntled family member of one of my clients. That happens sometimes."

"You've had vandalism before these incidents?" he demanded.

"Not vandalism. They usually yell at me in a parking lot or take me to court. Abusers don't like to let their targets go, Sergeant. I'm glad to say this is the first time someone has taken it this far."

He typed notes into his phone as she talked. Sliding the phone into his jacket pocket, he handed her his card. "I'll make an incident report. Get those cameras installed. Without video we can't do much. I need positive identification before I can make an arrest." With that he walked away, leaving her standing next to the broken bits in the driveway.

Time was getting away from her. She'd have to leave soon. She moved the biggest bits of the table from the driveway to the grass. She'd have to take care of the mess when she came home this evening. She got into the car and turned the key.

Nothing.

Great. Just great. She called AAA, then canceled all appointments before lunch.

The number of lost items began to register with her. Besides her grandmother's cabinet, she had lost her favorite jacket, the emergency kit from the trunk, a dozen CDs at $20 each, the time and expense of getting her car registration replaced... Angrily, she swiped away her tears. Why didn't he just STOP?

She had to think. Today's schedule was wrecked, and she had to let people know. Although the receptionist, Brenda, could take care of it, Haley usually liked to make appointments herself, so she knew what was happening. She dialed Brenda.

Daylon's truck pulled into the driveway while she was still in the car. He had stubble on his chin. His eyes looked red.

She got out of the car to speak to him. He scowled and came to her, shaking his head when he saw the crushed table. "I'm sorry, Haley," he said. "I should have had those cameras up for you."

Her heart gave a little squeeze. "Please, don't apologize. How is Scott?"

"He had a rough night. I stayed with him, so his wife could go home and take care of their children. As soon as she got back to the hospital, I left." He knelt down to look closer at the broken table.

"It was my grandmother's," Haley choked out. Hot tears made her eyes sting. "It's ruined. Completely ruined. Who could be so spiteful?"

Daylon lifted the cabinet top and looked at the tangled mass underneath. Rain glistened on the dark wood. Setting it gently down, he said, "It will never be a table again. You're right about that." He glanced up at her. "Since this is a family piece, I might be able to make something else from what's left. Would you mind

71

if I take a shot at it?"

"That would be wonderful. It's the only thing I have from her."

"No promises," he said, "but I'd like to give it a try…when I have time." He stacked the broken pieces onto the tabletop and picked the whole thing up. "I'll get those cameras installed today," he said and headed for the garage.

With the house on the left side of the driveway, the detached two-car garage stood at the end for easy entrance, although the garage mostly served as Daylon's shop. The driveway had room for at least four cars to park.

The AAA service truck arrived to jumpstart Haley's dead battery. Half an hour later, her car was back in working order. By then, lunchtime was minutes away, so she had more than an hour until her first afternoon appointment. Feeling damp and miserable, Haley changed into dry clothes and stretched out on her soft sofa. She closed her eyes to lose herself in a meditation audio and try to pull herself together. She felt shaky, off balance…violated.

The fear was real.

After all her professional training, her own personal development work, and all the energy healing she had been through, this morning took her back to the trauma of seeing her six-year-old brother, Andrew, fall through the ice. At the time, she was twelve years old and responsible to watch over her brother. She had stood by the edge of the pond, screaming hysterically while their friend's dad inched across the ice on his belly to pull Andrew out.

Her brother had survived. As an adult, he hardly remembered the incident.

Twenty-seven years later, the moment Haley realized her car

had been ransacked she had gone straight back to the abject horror of her life in danger.

She had four clients this afternoon. She had to get herself together, so that SORRY S.O.B. (whoever he was) DIDN'T TAKE THEM AWAY FROM HER, TOO.

She breathed, slow and deep...and released.

Somehow, she made it through the rest of the day without cancelling anyone else on her schedule. A little after six o'clock, she arrived home completely spent. Her upstairs veranda had two shiny white cameras, one pointed toward her door, the other pointed toward the driveway.

Daylon's truck was in the drive, but his curtains were drawn. She went upstairs and didn't see him until the following afternoon. Usually, she'd call Barb or Linda and fill them in. Tonight, she didn't have the energy and went straight to bed.

The next day, driving home from work, she had that familiar weary feeling she always had at the end of a long week, like her arms were twice as heavy as usual. The weather had turned warm, so she threw her coat into her backseat instead of putting it on. When she got out of the car, two robins flew up from the yard. The breeze felt good. She shook her head a little to loosen her hair and let its natural waves blow free around her cheeks.

Daylon's truck had the hood open. He was in the garage with the sliding door rolled up. "Hey," he called to her. "You got a minute?" He was rummaging inside a rusty toolbox that used to be red a long time ago. Now, it was a dull brown.

She stepped into the open doorway. "Hi. How's your son?"

He picked up a wrench, checked its size and laid it on the bench. "He's doing good. The doc says he might be able to move to the rehab center next week."

"He must have been pretty banged up."

73

"Three screws and a metal plate in his left leg." He grabbed a nearby rag to wipe motor grease from his hands. "He's alive, and he has a good chance of walking again. That's all good news." He held out a small cardboard box that had been on the bench.

"I took the liberty of picking up a camera for inside your car. You've got to have more coverage than just those two I put upstairs."

She glanced at the image on the cover but didn't touch the box.

"Another thing," Daylon went on, "let's set up a signal. If you hear anything in the middle of the night, pound on the floor and I'll be right up. While you call 911, stomp the hell out of the floor, okay?"

She nodded. "I need to get some rest, but I feel so edgy I doubt that's going to happen."

"Is there anyone you can stay with for a couple of days?"

"My best friend Barb lives a few doors down from where the murder happened. She's too close. My kids are both far away...." She shook her head. "All I want right now is my own place and peace and quiet."

"I get that. Believe me." He set the camera box down.

Suddenly cold, she pulled her coat on. "Tomorrow, I have to go out and replace the stuff he stole out of my car."

"What did he take?"

She spieled off the list.

"Wait a minute. Let me loan you a tire pump and a pair of jumper cables. I also have a jack around here somewhere. When all this straightens out, you can replace them and give mine back. There's no hurry." He paused half a second. "Consider that extra camera a loan, too. It was thirty bucks. That's not going to break me."

"I don't know how I can ever thank you. Not just for that. For everything."

"Hey, that guy is on my turf. I want him brought down as much as you do." He pulled out his cell phone. "Do you have your phone with you? Let's set up the camera app while you're here."

She pulled out her personal phone and handed it to him. Twenty minutes later, Haley stepped inside her front door and double locked it behind her.

She had a wine spritzer and put on meditation music, but she couldn't settle down enough to go to bed. Sometime after three a.m. she fell asleep while binge-watching Netflix. At dawn, she moved to the bed and stayed there until noon.

She was enjoying her last sip of coffee and her last bit of toast when someone tapped on her door. "Haley," Daylon called. "It's me."

When she opened, he said, "I put together some things for your car. Wanna take a look?"

"Let me grab some shoes and a coat. I'll be right out." She took an extra second to pull a brush through her hair and find her key fob before going down.

At the bottom of the stairs, he showed her a milk crate he had filled with several items. "I can put in the car webcam now, if you want."

"Sure." She hit the key fob to unlock the door.

He pulled the camera box from the crate and sat in the driver's seat to install it. His voice sounded muffled, so she moved closer. "The same app for the porch cameras will also pick up these two," he said. "See? This one device has one camera facing forward over the hood. The other camera has a wide angle to cover most of the inside of the car."

While he finished his adjustments, Haley set the crate inside the trunk.

Daylon called to her, "I don't know about your taste in music, but if you'd like to take a look at my CD collection, maybe you'll find something you'd like to borrow."

She headed back to him, chuckling a little. "Wow. Even CDs? You'll even loan me your CDs?"

He shot her a glance. "Why not? Unless you're a music snob... too good for Air Supply...Phil Collins…"

Her face lit up. "Hall and Oats?"

"Ha! Now you're talking." He got out of the car. "If you have time, come and see what you like. Borrow a few." He gave her a friendly grin. "You need cheering up. Blast them full volume upstairs. I don't care."

Replacing those silly CDs was the last thing on her mind right now, but she was curious, so she let him convince her.

Inside his apartment, he hit the power button on his stereo system before he pulled off his jacket. "Take a look," he said, nodding toward the double wire racks standing chin height next to the entertainment center. Time faded away as they looked through his collection.

When he put on "September" by Earth, Wind & Fire, Haley couldn't stop smiling. She gently moved to the music. Grinning, he grabbed her hand, and they were dancing. Daylon was better than she was. *Wow.*

Before tonight, she had rarely seen him smile. Come to think of it, she hadn't smiled much herself.

She caught a glimpse of the clock and gasped, "It's almost seven o'clock."

He grinned. "Let me take you out for a burger or something.

I'm not ready to call it a night. Are you?"

"A burger sounds amazing," she said, reaching for her coat. Sliding her arms into the sleeves, she said, "I needed this."

"We both did." He picked up his keys from a row of hooks in the kitchen and held the door open for her to go first. "The Englewood Diner okay?"

"Sure. They have great burgers."

He glanced at her. "Yes, they do."

They took his truck to the far edge of town. Fifteen minutes later, they slid into a scuffed red booth. The pattern on the gray Formica had worn off along the edges of the table, and the metal napkin holder had a dent. Still chilly, Haley kept her coat on. Daylon remained standing to pull off his red plaid coat while he greeted almost everyone in the place by name.

Haley ordered a double cheeseburger and iced tea. Daylon nodded at the waitress. "I'll have the same. Thanks, Mandy."

Feeling the comforting pressure of the seat against her back, Haley let out a slow sigh. She felt deliciously relaxed.

"I've lived in my apartment almost four years," Daylon said, his arms crossed and resting on the table.

Haley noticed the different hues in the blue plaid pattern on his flannel shirt. *That shirt is comfortable.* She wanted to touch it.

He went on, "The last renter above me was a guy who snored so loud, I could hear him downstairs."

"No." She shook her head. "You're not serious."

"I kid you not." He leaned back, so Mandy could set down their iced teas. "He was a hoarder. Sonia and Martin wanted him out because he was trashing the place, but he kept paying the rent, so they couldn't evict him."

"What happened?"

77

"It was a long, drawn-out process. They ended up taking legal action because their insurance company eventually refused to insure the house. They said the apartment was a fire hazard. The sheriff had to forcibly remove him. I spent the next four months remodeling the entire apartment—flooring, kitchen, bath—everything."

"It looks nice. You do good work."

He sipped tea. "You probably already know that my late wife, Alice, and Sonia were sisters. When Alice passed, Sonia and Martin offered me the apartment rent-free in exchange for maintaining their four rental properties. It's been a good thing. Medical bills completely wiped me out. I had to sell the house, and even then, I had to declare Chapter Eleven." He shrugged. "I'd do it all over again...at least I got to keep my truck."

"You said you're a private investigator? Do you take clients?"

He nodded. "It's more of a sideline. I keep my licenses up and that gives me access to information that's not open to the general public, mostly online stuff. A few people know about me and ask for help from time to time."

They ate and talked and ordered more tea and talked some more.

"I grew up on a farm near Scranton," he said. "That means I learned how to do plumbing, planting, carpentry, you name it, and just about anything under the hood of a truck. Dad ran beef cows and pigs. We also had a market garden and took produce to the sale on Saturday mornings.

"I got so tired of mucking around the barn and digging around in the dirt that I enlisted when I turned eighteen." He scoffed and shook his head. "Now, my favorite thing to do is dig in the dirt. Life is a funny thing, isn't it?"

Haley nodded. "I know. I wanted to be a researcher, so I majored in Biology at the same university where Salk discovered a vaccine for polio. Ended up getting married a few years later, so I got a Master's in Education and switched to teaching instead—you know, teachers are off when their kids are out of school—that old truism. Then I got a divorce, and my life completely changed. New degree, new town, new life."

"New apartment," he added. "Literally."

She chuckled. "I never thought of that."

After a while, Mandy stopped by their table, embarrassed. "We're about to close. Can I settle up your bill?"

Daylon raised his palm toward Haley. "I've got this."

She didn't object. She felt oddly mellow after a cheeseburger and iced tea.

When they reached the house, she got out of the truck and kept moving until she was two rungs up the stairs. She turned back to say, "Thanks for a fun time, Daylon. Good night," and kept climbing.

"Good night," he called after her.

She stepped inside her front door and flipped on the light.

Dad stood inside the living room doorway. He had a smirky kind of grin on his face. "So, Daylon, huh?" He nodded. "Not your type. At all."

Suddenly back to seventeen years old, she cried out, "Dad!"

He laughed. "I couldn't be happier. He's a great guy." He chuckled some more. "Notice, I'm not saying I told you so."

She took off her shoes and coat. "How's Linda?"

"Good. As good as can be expected, I mean." His grin disappeared. "I hear you've had some trouble. That's why I popped in."

She gave him the story of her car break in. "Daylon installed three cameras. Two on the verandah and one inside my car. I'll catch him."

"Looks like you already did," he murmured with a teasing smile. With that he disappeared.

She touched her heart, savoring the warm feeling her dad left her. Well…to be honest…it was already there before he popped in.

The next day was Monday, and she had promised Fleeta a visit. When she opened her door, a plastic canvas bag hung from her doorknob. It held six of the CDs they had danced to last night. Shuffling through them, Haley smiled all the way to the car. She slid Earth, Wind & Fire into the player and smiled all the way to the group home.

Parking, she switched off the music and took a moment to settle herself before she went inside. Pink climbing roses covered a trellis along the south side of the house, and a row of purple iris lined up in the front of the porch. As she passed, she heard bees happily humming over the roses.

The guard told her Fleeta was in the sitting room and let Haley find her own way. The hall opened into a wide sitting room with three sofas and four soft chairs. A TV hung high on the wall, like in a hospital room.

When Haley walked in, Fleeta was curled up on the end of a sofa watching an old rerun of *The Big Bang Theory*. Two older girls, sitting far apart from each other, were also watching the show.

When Fleeta saw Haley, she brightened and bounced to her feet. She wore soft lounge pants and a sweatshirt. She looked rested. "My dad's picking me up tomorrow!" she blurted out.

"Wonderful! That's the best news I've had all week!"

The closest girl made a loud *shushing* noise.

Haley leaned toward Fleeta and murmured, "Where should we go to talk?"

"Let's go to the dining room. No one's there right now," she said. She led the way to a long narrow room with three family-size tables and a serving window, now closed, connecting to the kitchen. Clinking and banging sounds of someone working in the kitchen came through the wall. They sat at the closest table.

Fleeta said, "Dad called me while I was still at breakfast. He said the paperwork should be ready this afternoon, and he'll be here tomorrow."

"It'll be just the two of you, right?"

Fleeta nodded. "I want to pick up my things from my room," she went on, suddenly serious. "All my clothes are there...and my iPad."

"I drove by your house, and it's sealed with police tape," Haley said. "Someone was mowing the lawn when I was there."

"Oh, yeah." Fleeta nodded. "That's Joey. He always does our yard. He has a special lawn mower he uses for racing. That thing can move."

"I saw it. He was going so fast, at first I thought he was going to crash."

"Joey always came over when we started the grill. We'd all sit outdoors and watch the stars." Her mouth puckered. Tears glistened.

"I'm glad you're going with your dad," Haley said to break the sad moment. "One thing, though. Since you're moving, you might be changing counselors." She handed Fleeta her card. "If you need anything at all, you can always call me. I'm still here for you."

She took the card and read it. "Okay."

Their meeting ended soon after that. Haley was headed down the hallway toward the front door when a *Whoosh* came over her, then a warm presence. It was Flo. She finally made contact.

Chapter Seven

When Haley arrived at work the next day, she spotted Cheri in the hall talking with her cousin, Sharon Marquette. About the same age, Cheri and her cousin were nothing alike. Sharon had the aura of an ancient Native American medicine woman. Along with her shamanic gifts, she was also a highly respected doctor of Chinese medicine. Her tinctures were famous in the area, and she had a steady stream of patients coming through Alexion's hallowed hall.

Haley greeted them both, then asked Cheri, "Do you have a moment?" Sharon excused herself and trudged to her office at the end of the hall, her shoes making soft shuffling noises.

Cheri looked ethereal in a powder blue dress of crinkled blue muslin. "Let's go into my treatment room," she said. Cheri's inner sanctum had tiny string lights along the edges of the ceiling and woven through her rattan shelving. Her acupuncture table stood on one side with an aromatherapy diffuser wafting out a combination of frankincense and patchouli. East Indian flute music played softly in the background.

Haley told her about feeling Flo's spirit the day before. "I've tried to reach out to her several times before because I have a feeling that whoever hurt Flo is also stalking me. But this is the first time I felt a clear connection." She gave Cheri the details about the car robbery. "I was hoping you might be able to find out more from Flo. To be honest, I'm scared he might come after me next."

82

Cheri closed her eyes and slowly inhaled—her way of checking in. She opened her eyes. "You're right. Flo is difficult to reach. We should go to the scene of her death."

"It's blocked off with police tape."

"If we can park in front of her house, that might be close enough."

Haley pulled out her phone to check her calendar. "I should be ready about four thirty today. Can you go after that?"

"That would be perfect. Do you mind if Frankie comes along? She loves this kind of thing."

Haley shrugged. "Sure." The back door opened. "That's mine." She touched Cheri's arm. "Thanks. See you later."

When Haley reached the hall, Val Jansen had just closed the door. Her blond hair was pulled up into a French braid that started on top of her head and reached the middle of her back. Her glow reminded Haley of Flo, a woman set free from the overpowering control of someone who did not have their best interest at heart.

Val smiled. "I brought you something." She held out a small plastic container. "Gluten-free, sugar-free brownies."

Haley's experience with gluten-free was less than five-star, actually more like one-star or zero-star. That must have shown on her face.

"It's made with a freshly baked apple, sweet potato and, believe it or not, avocado." She opened the lid to reveal three brownies. "Here, try one bite. If you don't like it, please say so right now, and I'll take them back home." She held out the container.

What could she do? Haley selected a small piece and took a small bite. A burst of sheer pleasure made her eyes close for an instant. She gasped, "Those are the creamiest brownies I've ever had in my life." She took the plastic container from Val's hands.

"I've got to have this recipe, and I'm not even gluten-free."

Val laughed. "See what I mean? I'm not gluten-free either. Those are so addictive I had to bring the last pieces with me, so I wouldn't finish the whole pan myself. Unfortunately, they aren't calorie-free."

When they settled in for their session, Val said, "Thanks for switching times for me. I have to drive to Scranton for an important meeting." She shivered. "I'm expecting good news, so I can't miss it."

"Tell me, what's new in your world?" Haley asked.

Val burst out, "Good news first! Jovan took a job in Canaburgh, so he's thirty minutes away now."

The size of a small college town, Canaburgh was the nearest cultural center with restaurants, theaters and sports facilities. The Canaburgh-Englewood Highway wound around the farms and over the streams of the Pennsylvania countryside for more than ten miles. A relaxing ride on a summer afternoon, on a snowy winter night that road was anything but relaxing.

Val lifted her chin and closed her eyes. "I'm so relieved. Even after the divorce, I could still feel him, like he was spying on me. I had to drive past our old house every time I came to town."

"It's time you go on with your life." Haley said, making a note. "How are things going with your family since you've been living with them?"

"I want to get my own place. If I get the promotion I'm expecting, maybe I'll move south a little to expand my sales reach and put more distance between me and Jovan."

Shortly after Val left, Haley had a text from her contact at Child Services. Fleeta's case had been transferred to a counselor specializing in adolescent care. They gave an email address for forwarding records. Haley was expecting that to happen, but she wished she'd had a chance to say good-bye.

The moment the last client of the day stepped out of her office, Haley quickly typed her final notes, closed her laptop and locked her office door. She found Cheri and Frankie in the kitchen sipping coffee, comfortable and relaxed as always.

When Frankie saw Haley, she smiled over the rim of her cup. "Hey, we're going ghostbusting!" She did a dance move with her long neck. Her blue feather earrings swayed in unison with her braids.

Haley grinned. The girl had style.

Cheri said, "Want coffee? It's decaf."

Haley saw the mostly filled pot on the coffeemaker. "I'll take half a cup to warm me up." She partially filled a blue mug with the saying, When You're Insane, You Don't Have to Explain. As she added cream and sugar, she said, "I hope this isn't a wild goose chase."

Cheri sipped the last of her coffee and dropped the cup into the tote for washing. Since the kitchen didn't have a proper sink, Cheri took the cups home every night and ran them through her dishwasher. "I have a good feeling about this afternoon," she said. She reached for her purse on the counter. "We're supposed to go right now. Bring your coffee. I'm driving."

They loaded into Cheri's white SUV. In the backseat, Frankie said, "I found a soft jean skirt at the thrift store yesterday. I'm going to pull out some of the threads and make some appliques."

"You should start an Etsy store," Haley said.

"I keep telling her that," Cheri remarked.

"I'm too busy having fun," Frankie retorted. "If I start a business, it will turn into work. Business plans, bank accounts…

blah!"

Cheri laughed. "I own three businesses, and I have fun," she said, braking for a yellow traffic light. "We need to work on your mindset."

"I need to work on my skirt!"

When they arrived at Flo's house, the police tape was gone. Cheri pulled her SUV into the driveway and right up to the garage door.

Frankie opened the back door. "I want to feel the energy."

They headed toward the covered sidewalk between the house and the garage. Before they reached it, Joey Everly appeared around the back of the garage. He was wearing the same brown bomber jacket he had on when he was mowing. He stared at them, frowning.

"Joey!" Frankie said, happy to see him. "How's it going?"

He pushed up his wire-rimmed glasses. His face was thin, his skin pale and soft as a baby's. With a wide grin, he called out, "Frankie! What are you doing here?"

She went on, smooth as silk, "Flo and Fleeta are friends of ours. We came to see if we can help in some way. Do they have family here?"

His eyes tightened with grief. "Is Fleeta okay? I've been so worried about her. They took her away the day it happened, and I can't see her."

Haley stayed quiet.

Cheri answered, "She's okay. She's safe."

He reached for a jangling ring of keys clipped to his wide leather belt. "I have a key to the house. Would you like to go in?" Not waiting for an answer, he unlocked the side door and waved his hand, as though urging them inside. Cheri was already stepping over the threshold. Haley followed. This felt too easy...or maybe too invasive.

Behind them, Frankie paused by the door. "Are you still going to the Steampunk Club, Joey?"

He nodded. "I'm working on a clock with big gears on the outside and a small face at the top. It's cool!" He pulled out his phone. "Here's a picture of it. This isn't mine. It's the pattern I found online. Mine is still a bunch of gears lying on my workbench."

Haley continued inside, and their voices faded. She had never been inside Flo's home before.

They went through a mudroom with dried dirt on the floor and a jumbled pile of boots on the rack. To their left was a half-bath. The doorway ahead opened into the kitchen with dark gray cabinets and smoky green tiles on the backsplash. The appliances were black and shiny. In the center of the kitchen stood a wide island with a prep sink and green marble countertop. That must be where she died.

Cheri stood near the island, eyes closed. She nodded a couple of times.

Haley felt into what Cheri was getting and got nothing. The kitchen area had gray laminate flooring with gray carpet over the rest of the great room. The back wall had a bank of windows showing most of the back yard. The fireplace had a TV over the mantle.

In a few minutes, Cheri opened her eyes and turned to Haley. "We can go now."

"Already?"

"I'll tell you about it in the car."

They found Frankie and Joey standing in the same place with their heads almost touching, still looking at photos on his phone.

Joey looked up. "Finished?"

Cheri nodded. "There's nothing much to see or do, is there?"

"I saw someone running out of the house and across the backyard," he said, pointing toward the gate in the wooden back fence. "He was wearing a dark hoodie. I couldn't see his face." He stroked down across his stubbled cheek with the back of his hand. "Flo and Fleeta were like my family. I can't believe they're gone."

On impulse, Haley pulled out her card and handed it to him. "If there's anything I can do, please give me a call."

Nodding, he took the card.

Frankie said, "I'll tell Conley we saw you. Give him a call, Joey. He'd like to see your project."

Nodding absently, Joey didn't reply. He stood there watching them leave, looking very alone.

The moment they closed the car doors, Frankie burst out from the backseat, "What happened?"

Cheri said, "Nothing dramatic. Let's get out of here and find a place to park, so I can fill you in."

Haley turned in her seat to face Frankie. "Wow. You were great with Joey. That was impressive."

"I see him around, but we don't really know each other. He's a friend, or maybe I should say an acquaintance, of Conley's." Conley was Frankie's best friend. After a short engagement, Frankie had friend-zoned the poor guy. Surprisingly, they still hung out. Young people did relationships very differently these days, a good thing from what Haley could see.

"He's a friend of Conley?" Cheri asked. Conley was Cheri's grandson.

Frankie nodded. "Right. It's steampunk, Cheri. They make things that look Victorian with all those gears and goggles and everything."

"Oh that." Cheri said. "I know Conley is crazy about that stuff, but I never knew he was in a club about it." She pulled into a side street and shut off the car. Turning in her seat, she said, "Okay, here's what happened." She took a breath. "Sometimes when a person dies suddenly and unexpectedly, they wander around for a while trying to figure out what's going on. Sometimes they think they are still alive."

Haley said, "They don't know they're dead? I've never heard of that."

Frankie said, "Ever see the movie, *The Others*?"

Cheri went on, "After the police finished their investigation, Flo's house sat empty. No family was there at all. Flo's spirit has been wandering around the house, waiting for Fleeta to come home from the slumber party. She was reaching out to find her. That must be when you sensed her, Haley."

"That's terrible," Haley said. "Poor Flo. Did she tell you who did this to her?"

"I got some images, but nothing we didn't already know. She's so upset about Fleeta that she didn't tell me much about how she died. She kept saying, 'He didn't mean it. He didn't mean it.' When I asked her for his name, I got no response. She went to be with Fleeta, and she's not going to talk to me for a while."

Haley touched Cheri's arm to interrupt her before she said more. "Flo isn't concerned about who hurt her?"

"I wouldn't say that," Cheri said. "Flo is just more concerned about her daughter right now. The energy is all about her daughter."

Haley sank back in her seat, deflated. "I was hoping for something more definite."

Cheri said, "In a week or two, I'll connect with her again. Or

89

maybe you can reach her yourself by then. Possibly she'll have more for us. Departed spirits tell us what's on their minds, not necessarily what we want to know." She started the car. "I think this went well. We made contact, and we did exactly what we told Joey we were going to do. We helped."

Frankie picked up her phone. "I'm going to text Conley about seeing Joey."

While she did that, Haley texted Fleeta: The police tape is off your house, so you can get your things now.

Fleeta: <giant smiley face> Thanks!

If Flo really had gone to stay with Fleeta, the girl would start feeling comforted and less alone.

The next day, Haley arrived at the Healing Circle to find the conversation humming about their ghostbusting experience in Flo's kitchen. Stepping aside so Martin could leave the room, Haley propped her dry umbrella in the corner next to the door. The day was so dreary she had brought it, in case.

She joined Barb on the couch in time to hear Linda ask Cheri, "Did you get a cold chill when she came through?"

While Cheri continued talking, Barb murmured to Haley, "Sounds like you had an adventure." She had sent out a group text that morning: No food today. Sorry. Now, relaxing on the sofa, she looked anything but sorry.

"It was over as quickly as it started," Haley said. "No bolts of lightning or anything. We didn't learn that much, not the most important thing anyway."

The meeting started with all six members present. Even Sonia had time to sit down because Martin was in the store today. As usual, they started by going around the circle with everyone sharing whatever was on their mind.

Sitting to the left of Cheri, Frankie said, "First, I'm so glad for my very good friends. I wish we could spend more time together."

Cheri smiled. "What? Old dinosaurs like us?"

Frankie sent her an affectionate smile. "I learned that spirits don't know everything, and their concerns in life follow them after death." She glanced at Haley. "They also don't talk in complete sentences."

Haley had reservations about that statement, but she kept it to herself.

Linda was next. "My soon-to-be-ex—whose name shall not be spoken—was served divorce papers yesterday afternoon." She slid back in her seat and looked into her coffee cup. "Another box ticked."

Sonia watched Linda's face. "You're pretty calm."

"That's my bedside manner. I'd like to pound the guy into next week." She adjusted her sweater. "It feels good to have him out of the house. No more fighting. No more tiptoeing around him, waiting for him to blow up at the kids."

Haley could feel Barb's energy spike. Barb had also married a cheater. She had come home unexpectedly to catch him making out with a woman on their couch. Without a word, Barb went upstairs and threw every single thing he owned out the bedroom window—laptop, files, everything. With a set to her jaw, Barb said, "Go get 'em, tiger."

A sympathetic chuckle went through the group.

Haley gave them a quick update on her stalking situation and asked that everyone stay alert for anyone hanging around outside Alexion Acupuncture. Talking about it put a tight knot in her stomach. Her client sessions kept her focused on other people's problems, so she didn't have to think about her own. These reports brought everything back to the surface. She was glad to get back to work.

Before she left for the day, she received a text from Daylon: I have news. Stop by my place when you get home?

That knot in her stomach grew a little tighter, if that were possible. When she knocked on his door half an hour later, Daylon opened it immediately. He was wearing the same faded jeans, blue flannel shirt and white socks as always. Did he wash them at night and put them back on?

She stepped inside, already wishing for her sweatpants. "What is it, Daylon?"

He looked somber. "Pauly Hammond overdosed last week."

Chapter Eight

Haley gasped. "What happened? Is he okay?"

He stepped back to invite her inside. "He was released yesterday. I saw him in a wheelchair yesterday afternoon while I was at the hospital. I spent this morning doing some digging and called a friend who works the 911 dashboard." He tilted his head toward the living room. "Please come in and sit down. This might take a while."

She stepped inside and sat on the lounge chair with her trench coat still on. Daylon took a seat on the leather sofa and continued, "My friend went through the 911 call recordings. Around six on the evening of May 13, Pauly Hammond overdosed on some substance. I don't have all the details, but someone found him in time to call an ambulance." He stood up to grab a legal pad from the dining room table. "He was admitted to the hospital around the same time as my son was." He handed his notes to her. "Check this out."

She glanced at the notes and handed them back. "We need to go over this, but I'm desperate to get out of these clothes. Can I come back later? Do you have plans for tonight?"

He laughed out loud. "Haley, I never have plans. You can stop asking that any time now. I'll leave the door unlocked. Come back when you're ready."

She chuckled and headed for the door. A few minutes later, she let herself back into his place, carrying a plastic food container and a paper bag. Daylon was pulling leftovers out of the fridge. A gallon jug of iced tea sat on the counter. She held up the container. "I brought the rest of the beef stew I made yesterday."

He gave her a delighted glance. "I'll see your homemade stew with yesterday's restaurant lasagna and raise you some Greek salad I made myself." He popped the lid on her container and looked inside. "Mmmm...As for me, I'm having beef stew."

She held out the paper bag. "Dinner rolls."

While the microwave hummed, Daylon spread his files and notes across the end of his dining table where they could reach them while they ate.

Haley paused to look at a family picture on the wall—a much younger Daylon with a glowingly beautiful woman and a boy around twelve years old. They were all blond, wearing black turtleneck shirts and black pants.

"My family," he said.

Haley lingered on each face. They looked so happy.

"That picture was taken about fifteen years ago. Alice got diagnosed when Scott was nineteen, and she lived until he was twenty-three. She got to see him graduate from college." He nodded toward a cabinet door. "Plates are in there. Glasses, too. Would you mind setting us up?"

She moved around the kitchen and let comfortable silence fill the room. From the white Formica counters to the brown wood cabinets, this kitchen had been around for at least forty years. The stainless-steel refrigerator looked like it had been recently replaced.

Daylon lifted a steaming bowl of stew from the microwave and set the lasagna in its place. Haley dished the salad into two bowls.

When they sat down, she said, "I feel like the rug has been

pulled out from under me. I was so certain Pauly was the stalker. Who else could it be?" She pulled the pad with the timeline toward her and leaned on her hand, looking it over.

"That's a problem with investigation," Daylon said. "Once you get focused on a solution, any alternatives magically disappear from your mind." He took a bite of beef stew and sent her a long glance, impressed. "This is good!"

She smiled. "Thanks! It's a crockpot special. Anyone could do it." She sipped tea. "When did you see Pauly in a wheelchair?"

"Yesterday. I went to the hospital because my son, Scott, was transferred to a rehab facility. I was in the elevator going down with my hands full with Scott's stuff. The entourage with Scott's wheelchair was a ways behind me, so I was in the elevator alone. When I got to the lobby, I almost fell over Pauly Hammond in a wheelchair. I stood there and watched him go into a waiting ambulance for transfer. I'm not sure where he was headed."

She jabbed at an olive, disgusted. "Well, that's it then."

"What do you mean?" He dipped a buttered roll into the thick stew and took a big bite.

"No more checking into who killed Flo. It's too dangerous."

He nodded. "I'm with you there. Do you know of anyone else connected to Flo who might come after you?"

She considered, then slowly shook her head. "She was already divorced when I met her. After she passed, I spoke to her ex on the phone. He didn't seem to have any particular animosity toward me. He had only one thing on his mind—taking care of his daughter."

Popping the last bit of roll into his mouth, Daylon wiped his hands on a napkin and turned to a fresh page on the legal pad. He picked up the pen. "We've got too many things going on at once. It's too confusing. Let's sort them out. He wrote *Stalker* on top of the sheet. "Your first incident was…"

"The dead rat," she said.

"You had a dead battery before that," he said.

"At the time, I thought that was a fluke." She glanced at Daylon. "Maybe it *was* him. The repair shop couldn't find anything wrong."

"Okay, just for giggles, let's go with the battery as the first incident. Do you know the date?"

She reached for her purse on his coffee table. It had a wrought iron frame with a thick glass top. "I keep my receipts in here." Shuffling through a stack of papers, she found the one she was looking for. "April 21. It probably happened in the early hours that morning."

He made a note.

"The dead rat… I don't have paper for that one. It was a couple of weeks later." She shuffled more papers. "The car break in… May 14. Here's the Triple-A receipt for service." She showed him the page. "That's almost three weeks later. Why the gaps?"

"Maybe he doesn't live around here."

"Maybe he was sick, or maybe his mother-in-law came to visit…" She spooned lasagna into her empty salad bowl.

Daylon chuckled. "Maybe he stubbed his toe on the coffee table and couldn't put on his shoe."

"Maybe his pet iguana bit him on his pinky." Haley laughed. "How far do you want to take it? We could go on all night."

He started a column on the right side of the page. "Let's jot down all the maybe's… the serious ones." He listed:

- Lives out of the area
- Had houseguests and couldn't get away
- An injury that kept him inside

"How about this one?" he said. "His job takes him out of town."

"Who do I know that works out of town?" She paused to run through her list of possible stalkers. "I can't think of anyone."

When he finished the list, he said, "Before we move on, is there anything else about Flo's death that might have bearing on your stalker? Anything at all?"

She twisted her lips. "You'll probably think I'm crazy, but I might as well get this out there now." She drew in a breath to give herself time to find a place to begin, certain that the practical, logical Marine officer sitting next to her wasn't going to take this well. "Sometimes, I get messages from the other side. From people who have crossed over, I mean."

"You mean like a medium?"

She nodded. "I don't hold seances or anything like that. I rarely even tell anyone about it, but," she winced, "sometimes I get messages."

He had that humorous glint in his blue eyes. "White figures standing at the end of your bed?"

She chuckled. "I majored in biology, and I taught high school science for ten years. In those days, I had a special word for weird people who believed in ghosts. I called them whack-a-doo."

He chuckled.

Haley went on, "That is, until my father died four years ago. I had a sense that he was near me, and sometimes words popped into my mind."

"So, you got a message from Flo?"

"More like her presence. I couldn't get anything specific, so I asked Cheri Alexion for help. Do you know her?"

"Red hair and she wears long skirts?"

97

Haley nodded.

"I've seen her around...mostly at the bookstore. I don't remember ever speaking to her."

"She's much better at talking to departed spirits than I am. She went with me to Flo's house to see if we could pick up a message about what happened. When Cheri asked who had hurt her, Flo kept saying, 'He didn't mean it. He didn't mean it,' and then she disappeared. That's all Cheri got." She watched his reaction. "That's odd, don't you think?"

He frowned. "I'm the wrong person to ask that question. Everything you're telling me is odd. So, what you're saying is that you believe the perp is someone who cares about Flo and didn't intend to hurt her."

Haley shivered. "That sounds like her husband to me. He was frantic about his daughter, Fleeta, and totally distraught about what happened to Flo. Of course, that would be natural whether he was the one who hurt her or not." She pressed her fingertips against her forehead. "My head is starting to ache."

He turned to a clean page on the legal pad. "I agree that Flo's case doesn't seem to have any bearing on your stalker. Let's go back to the beginning of the stalking, to those guys you had me do a background check on." He looked through the stack of papers. "I have the reports here somewhere." Papers skittered across the table.

"Ever hear of a thumb drive and Excel?" she asked.

He shot her a glance. "I trust paper. You can't click Delete on paper." More flipping pages. "Here they are. Harry, Rob and Eli. The Three Stooges."

"You're not wrong," she said. "Three Stooges is a good way to put it. My personal favorite is Eli because he was the last one I dated. If the other two had decided to stalk me, they took a while to get started."

He wrote *Romance* on top of the clean page. "Let's get to Eli last because I have the most information on him. First up, Harry Grimes. I got nothing on Harry. My background check came up blank. He never had so much as a speeding ticket, not even a parking ticket."

"He was a retired schoolteacher whose wife had died two years before I met him. He didn't really want to date. His kids pushed him into it. One of them set up his profile and connected him with a few women to 'get the ball rolling.' His words, verbatim."

Daylon spoke as he wrote, "Rob Kerry."

"Rob was a really nice guy. I liked talking to him. He was tall, athletic, and he had a nice voice. He could have read audiobooks for a living."

"What did he do for a living?"

"He was retired from some kind of corporate job. He never said which company. He liked to hang out in graveyards, looking at tombstones and seeing the family history of people from years ago. A little weird. But nice."

"Did he talk to ghosts, too?"

"Actually, we never discussed it."

"When did you end things with him?"

"About a month before the stalking started. Let's see...I had two first dates the same week, one with Rob and one with Eli Loomis. I had second dates with both of them the following week. That's when I friend-zoned Rob. He was disappointed but overall, pretty philosophical about it. He said something like, 'You win some, you lose some.'"

"And when did that happen?"

She pulled out her personal phone to check her calendar. "It was around March 30th. I dated Eli for about a month after that, not long enough to have him pick me up at home. If he came here, he would have looked up my address."

Daylon sipped iced tea and set the glass down. "Yeah, those first two guys would have acted sooner. Okay, tell me about Eli." He wrote down *Eli Loomis*.

"We went over most of this before," Haley said. "Mid-forties. He had a sort of Mediterranean look with thick black hair that had a bit of a wave to it. He was always joking.

"At first, I thought he had a jolly personality, but once I got to know him, I started seeing the negative side of him, and I didn't like it. His jokes were mostly cynical and demeaning, not really funny."

She paused for a second. "This might be important...he was married three times. When I met him, he had been single for seven years, at least according to what he told me."

"That's quite a turnover...three marriages by the time he was around forty? And his last wife got a restraining order," Daylon finished.

"What bothers me was the way he treated me when I broke things off with him. We were having dinner at Rubio's in Canaburgh at the time. I tried to be kind about it. I told him that I had enjoyed our time together, but we weren't a good fit."

"That place has great seafood," Daylon said. "I love their cioppino."

She gasped. "Me too! That's what I ordered that night, as a matter of fact. When I told Eli it was over, he stared at me with this hateful look in his eyes, then he threw his napkin on top of his food and left the restaurant. I had to pick up the check." She grinned, mischievous. "I stayed and finished my food. No way was I going to miss out on fresh hot cioppino because he was an ass."

"What does he do for a living?"

"Stocks, investments…" She shrugged. "I'm not really sure. He traveled overseas quite a bit."

"Okay, so he would have a reason to be out of town and not come back to harass you for a while. I'm liking this guy more and more. If he has nosy neighbors, I might get more information." He scribbled notes. "We need to get his whereabouts. That will take some work, but I can pull in some favors. The first place to start is his latest ex. I wonder what she would say about that restraining order."

Haley's mouth tensed. "I need to hire you. This is taking your time, gas money…"

He grinned at her in his boyish way and dropped the legal pad onto the stack of papers with a *thwack*. "I'll put it on your tab," he said, standing. "In the meantime, how about some Lynyrd Skynyrd?"

He was wearing that comfortable blue flannel shirt. How could she say no?

Two hours later, she sat in her chair at the table and drained her glass of iced tea. All the ice had melted. Daylon filled her glass with ice and pulled the jug from the fridge to give her a refill.

She checked her phone. "It's almost nine, and I have to work tomorrow. Let me help you clear this away."

Sipping from his own cold glass, he leaned back against the kitchen counter. "Clear what away? Two plates and two glasses? I have a dishwasher."

She drank more tea like she couldn't get enough.

"I haven't had this much fun in years," he said. "I hope we can do it again."

She smiled as she put on her coat. "I'm sure we will. See you later." She quickly let herself out before he could say more. Her heart was thumping a little. Was that fear? Anxiety? Anticipation? *Self-analysis will make you crazy*, she told herself, and forced those thoughts out of her mind.

Half an hour later, she pushed open the glass door on her walk-in shower to reach for her towel. She stepped onto the pink memory foam mat to finish toweling her feet dry. Her ex-husband hated pink and wouldn't let her have it in the house. Now she had it everywhere from the pink peonies covering her sofa to the pink towels in her bathroom. Pink made her happy.

Her phone chirped, but she took her time checking it. When she did, she stopped in her tracks. That ping had come from her online scheduler. A new client had booked an appointment on Friday afternoon, the day after tomorrow. His name was Joey Everly

Chapter Nine

Joey Everly arrived for his appointment exactly on time. He had downloaded the intake papers from her website, and he handed them to Haley, every line neatly filled out. His look reminded Haley of someone in the clergy—super clean with baby-smooth skin and sandy brown hair, cut short with a receding hairline.

"Can I get you some water?" Haley asked. "Or maybe some tea?"

"I'm good," he said. He took a seat on her white sofa. His legs were so long, his shins touched the coffee table. Haley pulled it toward her a little to give him more room. He pushed up the bridge of his wire-rimmed glasses in a nervous gesture.

Scanning his paperwork, she was surprised to see that he was twenty-eight years old. She thought he had recently graduated from college. She dropped the pages to her lap and gave him her full attention. "What brings you in today, Joey?"

He cleared his throat. "At my monthly doctor appointment, I told her about my nightmares. She said I should see a counselor, so I made the appointment."

"Who did you see?" Haley looked down at his pages.

Before she spotted his doctor's name, he said, "Dr. Linda Blankenship."

That wasn't a surprise. Around this town, almost everybody was Linda's patient. Haley read that Joey was taking medication for anxiety.

"How is your anxiety? On a scale of one to ten?"

Expressionless, he said, "Since all that happened...you know, with Flo...it stays about a seven. It used to be a four. Dr. Linda increased my dose."

"You've had a shock, Joey," Haley said. "I'm sorry you've had to go through this."

"I heard Fleeta screaming and screaming, so I ran into the house...and there was Flo...on the floor. I tried to wake her up." His voice drifted off. He stared at a spot on the wall, despair puckering his forehead. "I still can't believe it really happened. It seems like a bad dream I can't wake up from."

"Tell me about your nightmares. Do they happen every night?"

He nodded. "Sometimes twice a night. I wake up sweating and shaking. Sometimes I'm sweating so much I have to shower and change my bed."

"Is it always the same?"

Plucking at his pants leg, he nodded. "It starts out that I'm in Flo's yard, weeding the front flower bed. The plants turn into vines and wrap around me, so I can't move. They squeeze tighter and tighter until I can't breathe. Then I wake up."

"Do you take anything to help you sleep?"

"I started taking something I picked up at the pharmacy. I can't remember the name."

"Sometimes sleep aids cause nightmares. You might want to stop taking them for a few nights to see if that helps." She made a note. "Do you journal?"

He shook his head.

"Sometimes writing for a few minutes each day helps get troubling thoughts out, so they don't keep repeating in your mind."

He focused on her, intrigued. "I could try that. I'm a writer, but I've never thought about journaling." He nodded. "I'll try that."

"You're a writer?"

"I've written two steampunk novels," he said, "...and two people bought them." He suddenly chuckled and his whole face lit up for a brief second. "Well, more than two, but you get the picture."

When she asked about his parents, he told her that his parents were nearly forty years old when he was born. They were loving parents, but Joey was bullied mercilessly at school. Instead of socializing with other kids, he tinkered at his father's workbench in the basement. That's how he got interested in steampunk.

"Dad worked with me," he said, gazing at a place over Haley's head, remembering. "He taught me how to be a maker." He paused and took a breath. "Dad died two weeks after my college graduation," he said. "So, I came home and stayed with Mom."

"What was your major?" Haley asked.

"History," he said. "Do you know how many jobs are waiting out there for a history major? I tell people I came home to stay with my mom, and I did. That's no lie. But I also had no prospects. I ended up working for a landscaping company and doing odd jobs for people in the neighborhood. Some good that history degree turned out to be."

At the end of the session, Haley gave him a printout of things to do when he felt anxiety. They made an appointment for the next week.

After he left, she sat a moment before beginning her notes. Her own grief at Flo's passing welled up inside her. For the first time in her life, Flo was genuinely happy. She had broken the cycle of dependence and was taking a stand for herself in many ways. Haley felt a rush of anger. It wasn't fair that Flo was gone. She closed her eyes and drew in a slow breath. In a moment, she started typing.

Closing her laptop a few minutes later, she picked up the snowflake fridge magnet she kept on her desk and ran it over her prime meridians to clear herself of the intense energy still lingering. Her next client would arrive in seven minutes.

She finished client meetings at three and spent an hour filing insurance. Feeling like she was playing hooky, she pulled into her driveway a few minutes after four.

Immediately, Daylon's door opened. He leaned out to say, "I'm about to make a call. You might like to hear it. Want to come down after you change?"

She felt her brow wrinkle. "Who are you calling?"

"You'll see." He closed the door.

Cheeky man. Chuckling to herself, she continued up the stairs. This was getting to be a habit... but she wasn't complaining.

She braced herself before opening her door. Dad was inside. She could feel him. She smiled and pushed it open to see him in the hall.

He grinned at her.

"I thought you were here," she said, closing the door and turning the deadbolt. She set her purse on the lounge chair. "I'm here to change and go back out."

"Hot date?"

"Not really. Just down to Daylon's to work on the investigation."

"Hot date," he said, nodding. "I just wanted to say hi. Don't let me slow you down."

She gave him an arch look. "You're not coming in while I

106

change."

He began to fade. "TTYL. I learned that from Linda's kids..." and he was gone.

She smiled as she pulled her green velour sweatsuit from the drawer. Who would have ever thought her dad was such a fun guy? He hardly talked at all when he was alive. Now, he talked non-stop.

She heard his voice in her mind. *This is how I really was all the time. Life just got in the way.*

Holding her sweatshirt to cover her bare midriff, she said, "Dad!"

His laughter echoed. *I'm on the roof, silly. I don't have to be there to talk to you.*

Shaking her head and laughing in spite of herself, Haley finished dressing.

A few minutes later, she opened Daylon's door without knocking. "Hey, what are you up to?" she asked, joining him at the dining table.

"I'm about to call Eli's ex-wife number three." He nodded toward the chair next to him. "Sit there and don't move or make a sound. I'm going to put the phone on speaker. This will be fun."

What the...? She sat.

In a deep, expansive voice, Daylon said, "Hello, my name is David Perry. I'm calling from the University of Pennsylvania. We are conducting a survey for Victim Advocacy as part of a Master's program, following up with people who filed restraining orders in this state over the last ten years. The survey takes five minutes. It's only a few questions. Can you help us out?"

A soft, feminine voice hesitantly murmured, "Okay."

"You filed a restraining order against...," short pause to

shuffle papers near the phone, "...a Mr. Eli Loomis about seven years ago, is that correct?"

"Yes."

"What was your reason for filing?"

"We were going through a divorce, and he kept coming here to fight with me. Once he banged so hard on the door, he broke the window. I called 911, and the officer told me to file a restraining order. So, I did."

"Did you hear from Victim Advocacy at that time?"

"Yes. They called to say I can contact them if I need help, whatever that meant. I never called them back."

"Thank you for your time," he said. "That's all I need. Bye." He hung up. Then, he laughed. His upper body jiggled as he leaned back in the chair.

Haley stared at him with pretend dismay. "It's a little disturbing how good you are at that. And how much fun you have doing it."

Coughing, he picked up his iced tea and drank. In a moment, he said, "We got lucky. She picked up." He flipped a page on his notepad and wrote for a second. Finally, he said, "Eli has a temper."

Haley sounded doubtful. "I know he's the most likely one to stalk me, but I've been thinking... Why stalk me after dating only five or six weeks? That part doesn't make sense to me. We weren't dating long enough for him to be that invested. All he had to do was swipe left on me and find someone else." She stood up. "This has been fun, but I'm really tired. Somebody had me on my feet dancing for hours last night. I have to go home now." She lightly touched his shoulder. "See you later."

That weekend was Haley's first real weekend off in a month. She determined to make the most of it and be as lazy as she pleased for two long, gorgeous days. And she did.

The next Healing Circle was sparse with only Cheri, Barb and Haley present. Cheri wore Frankie's latest creation, a kerchief skirt in varying shades from cream to burnt sienna to mahogany, layered to look like she wore three skirts with a dozen points swishing around her shins.

Barb brought a salad with small containers of cubed ham and shredded cheese on the side, so Cheri could enjoy the meal with them.

While Haley was dishing up greens, Barb said, "These are fresh from my restaurant garden." Barb rented a dedicated plot from a local farmer who delivered fresh vegetables to the restaurant daily.

Haley bit into a piece of lettuce. "Oh my God," she said, chewing. "This is incredible."

Barb said, "They were still in the ground four hours ago."

"I'm glad you brought plenty," Haley said, piling more on top of what she already had on her plate.

Cheri was in vegan paradise. After her first bite, she didn't speak for a full five minutes. Finally, she said, "After everyone has a chance to share today, let's make a crystal grid and spend about fifteen minutes in silent meditation. We need it. With a small group, we'll have time."

Haley said, "Do you have a grid with you?"

"Do you need to ask?" She set her plate on the coffee table and reached into a pocket of her skirt. "I wasn't sure we'd use it, but I had an impulse to bring this along." She pulled out a folded blue cloth, opened it and placed it on the coffee table to show the Flower of Life printed in white. From the same pocket, she pulled out a dozen small crystals in various colors and carefully placed them on the Flower of Life.

Sitting together in meditation amplified the effect. Haley focused on her breathing, and reveled in the calming of her body and emotions. In place of the stress, a beautiful silence grew, a sense of peaceful gratitude. She loved these meditations. Reluctantly, she returned to the room when their time was up. This is why Haley kept attending the Healing Circle.

When the meeting was over, Barb took her phone off airplane mode and immediately got a text. She glanced at it. "Oh, shoot!" she burst out.

Haley said, "Everything okay?"

"Zoe has to pull a double shift. Two people are out sick. We have tickets to see *How to Succeed in Business Without Even Trying* at the community theater tonight. We were looking forward to it." She frowned. "Shoot!"

"So sorry," Haley said. "That would have been a great time."

Barb stacked plates into her carryall. She hated eating off of paper plates, so she always brought thick white crockery from the cafe. She glanced at Haley. "Say, would you like to go with me? I may as well use the tickets. The alternative is a night at home alone eating cold spaghetti." She lifted the strap of the carryall over her shoulder.

"Sure. I'll play second fiddle. I'm not proud."

Barb laughed. "We have reservations at Rubio's, so we'll need to leave Englewood by five thirty. Will that be okay?"

Haley nodded. "What a treat! Thanks, Babe."

"You can thank me by driving," Barb replied. "Pick me up at my house. I want to change. Okay, *mija*?"

"I'll be there with bells on. I might put on some clothes, too."

After her last client, Haley went home, freshened her makeup and changed into black palazzo pants with a silky beige tunic top and sparkly jacket. Dad didn't appear, but Daylon did. He came out of his apartment as she reached the sidewalk.

"Oh, you're going out," he said, a little disappointed. "I thought you might want to share dinner. I ordered chicken parm from Georgio's."

"How about a rain check?" she said. "My friend Barb asked me to go with her to the theater. Her date bailed at the last minute."

He grinned. "Sounds like a plan. Have a great time."

The minute Haley pulled into the driveway, Barb hurried out. She had on a ruffled red skirt that billowed with each step. In sixty seconds, they were on their way.

Haley announced, "I'm ordering salmon tonight, my second-best favorite at Rubio's.

Barb laughed. "You're such a foodie. That's why I love you."

The meal was fabulous, and the community theater was raucous. After laughing for almost two hours straight, they were feeling pumped on the way home.

As soon as Haley turned onto the Canaburgh-Englewood road, red-and-blue lights flashed behind them.

"What the...?" Barb said, turning around. "It's a cop."

"I wasn't speeding," Haley said. "Maybe he'll go around." She pulled off the road and stopped.

He pulled in behind her and got out of his car. At the back of her car, he leaned down. A moment later, he shone a flashlight through the car as he walked up toward Haley's door. The light shone into Haley's eyes. "License, ma'am?"

She winced under the glare. All she could see of him was his legs. "What did I do wrong?" She handed him what he asked for.

He shined his light on her license. "Do you have a cell phone in the car?"

Haley hesitated.

"Ma'am?"

"Yes," she said.

"May I see it, please?"

Confused, Haley handed it to him.

He looked at it, pressed the screen a few times, then handed it back. "We're spot checking for texting while driving," he said. "You're in the clear on that, but you have a tail light out. This is a courtesy. Be sure to get that light fixed before someone else stops you. Have a good night." He headed back to his car, put out the flashing lights and took off before Haley got her belongings put away.

Barb said, "That was weird."

"More than weird. Who ever heard of a cell phone check?" She put the car in gear and waited for an approaching car to pass before pulling into the road. "How did I get a broken light? I'd certainly remember if I hit something, and I haven't."

When they pulled into Barb's neighborhood, Barb said, "Zoe gets off at eleven. We're going to get there about the same time."

"It was a great evening, Babe," Haley said. "I'm sorry Zoe couldn't make it, but I'm really glad for the night out with you."

"You should come for dinner," Barb said. "Let's set up a time real soon, okay?"

Haley eased her car into the driveway and hit the unlock button. With a quick good-bye, Barb stepped out, her red skirt glowing in the headlights.

Driving home, Haley wondered if Daylon was still awake. Probably too late to tell him about the tail light tonight. Her head felt heavy with fatigue. She needed to get to bed anyway.

When she arrived home, Daylon came to his living room window. Haley waved to him, and he came to his door.

"Sorry to bother you so late," she said.

He looked concerned. "Did something happen?"

"Would you mind coming out to see my tail light? I got pulled over tonight because of a broken tail light. I have no idea when that could have happened."

"Let me get my shoes." He came out wearing his red jacket

and carrying a flashlight.

The break was so small that Haley said, "How did he even see that? I can hardly see it standing right here."

"Turn on your lights," Daylon said.

When she got back, she saw a small beam of white light coming from the red lens.

"It's an old trick," Daylon said, "Break a corner of a tail light, and you can follow someone without losing them."

She lost her breath. "Someone is following me?"

"I have some clear red tape in my toolbox. It's a quick fix for something like this."

"Don't do it tonight, Daylon," she said. "It's too late. Tomorrow is soon enough." Maybe because it was late or maybe she was tired, her face twisted and tears welled up.

He drew her into a hug.

"I'm not a crier," she said, sniffling into his shoulder.

"Everyone has their breaking point." He felt so solid and calm. "You've held up longer than most."

She let herself relax into him for a few more seconds. He felt so good. Pulling away, she wiped her eyes with both hands. "I need to go up to bed. I have seven clients tomorrow." With a quick good night, she headed upstairs.

Within minutes, she fell into a deep sleep and didn't move until four in the morning when her personal phone chirped. Worried that something might have happened to one of her children, she picked up her phone to read the text:

You're going to be sorry real soon.

Chapter Ten

She had to call the police. Should she wait until morning and end up cancelling appointments because they stayed so long? Or should she call them now and get no more sleep until time to go to work?

In the end she decided she wasn't going to get back to sleep anyway. She might as well call now. She pressed 911 and told the operator, "I have a stalker who has been vandalizing my car. Now, I just got a threatening text." She verified her address and hung up the phone.

She changed her pajamas for her green sweats and ran a comb through her hair. It was starting to look shaggy. Time to make an appointment with the hairdresser. She dropped the comb and headed to the living room.

She hovered near her front window, peering through the blinds when Dad appeared near her shoulder. "Why are you up at this hour?"

"I got a threatening text, so I called the police."

He frowned. "No one is out there. What can the police do?"

"I have to make a report anyway. You know, to build a case."

"I'm going outside," he said.

The motion-activated light in the yard came on. A police officer got out of his patrol car. He didn't come up right away but walked around the perimeter of the building and garage. Her phone said it was 4.23 a.m.

When the officer approached the stairs, Daylon came out of

his apartment and spoke to him. Under the glow of the security lights, misting rain formed a haze around them. It was Sgt. Kirk. He towered over Daylon by at least six inches, and Daylon wasn't a short guy.

Both men looked up at the security cameras on Haley's verandah, and Daylon pointed to her car. In a moment, Daylon returned to his apartment, and Sgt. Kirk came upstairs.

Haley waited until she heard a knock before she opened the door. She told him what happened and handed him her phone. "This is the text," she said. "I don't give out my personal number to anyone. I have no idea how he got it."

"I talked to your neighbor. He showed me the cameras. You're doing all the right things." He took a screenshot of the sender's number and the text. "I'll check on the number. If we get a name, I'll let you know." He sent himself a text from her phone, and his phone played the default four-note tune. "Now you have my number in your phone. Text me directly if anything else happens that's non-emergency, okay? You won't have to go through 911 for that."

She took her phone back. "Thank you."

The moment the policeman reached his patrol car, Daylon texted her: Are you going back to sleep?

She spoke into the phone to text back: No. Too keyed up.

Daylon: Come down. I'll make you breakfast. We need to talk.

Haley: I'll shower and be down in thirty minutes. I'll text when I'm opening my door. I'm a little spooked.

At quarter to six, Daylon stood near the stairs when she reached the sidewalk. He didn't say anything until he closed his door behind them. His mouth was tense. "I'm a little upset with you," he said.

115

Her eyebrows went up. "Why?"

"You didn't bang on the floor when you called the cops."

"At four in the morning?"

"I don't care what time it is." His voice intensified. "If it ever happens again—which I hope it doesn't—bang on the damn floor. I saw flashing lights, and I thought something awful had happened to you."

She shuddered. "I think I'm in shock. I'm shivering."

"Sit in the lounge chair. I'll get you a blanket." He came back with a quilt and pushed it around her. "I have coffee ready."

"Cream and one sugar," she said. She leaned back and closed her eyes. She wanted to think, but her head felt like it was stuffed with cotton. The quilt felt good. Daylon handed her a cup of steaming coffee.

"How do you like your eggs?" he asked. "We can talk while I cook. Tell me about how you got stopped last night."

"Eggs over easy," she said. "Last night, I went to Canaburgh with my friend, Barb. We saw a play at the community theater and headed home around ten fifteen. I had just turned onto the Canaburgh-Englewood road when a policeman pulled me over."

"You were driving?" he said over the sizzle of frying bacon.

"Yes. It was weird. I wasn't doing anything wrong. He said he was spot checking for texting while driving. After that, he mentioned my tail light was broken."

"Did he give you a ticket?" He turned the bacon with kitchen tongs. "Toast?"

"Yes, to the toast. One piece. Thanks." She sipped coffee. "Since I wasn't texting, he said it was a courtesy stop and let me go. He didn't even give me a warning for the broken light."

"Did you check the video from your car camera? Maybe it shows how the light was broken."

She gasped. "I never thought of it…no…actually, I didn't have time." She ran her fingers up the back of her neck and through the underside of her hair. "Everything has been happening so fast."

He stepped closer, his expression softer. "I'm so glad you're okay. Seeing the police scared the crap outta me."

"If there's a next time, I'll wake you. I promise." The lounge chair felt good. Her eyes drifted closed. Dad's voice came in softly, *See, he is a good guy.*

Daylon went back to the stove. "Do you mind if I have access to your car's video app?" When she didn't answer, he went on, "If that bothers you, don't worry about it. I just thought I could look at it while you're at work."

She opened her eyes. "Not at all. I'll give you the password."

He wrote it on the shopping list pad hanging on the fridge, then quickly scooped the bacon out of the pan. The toaster popped. "Here's your plate, coming up." He set a perfect breakfast plate on the table. Bacon crisp, eggs just right and golden toast, all neatly arranged.

Haley brought her coffee cup to the table and immediately pushed the toast to the center of the plate, piled bacon on top of the toast and scooted the eggs on top of that. She cut through the stack with her fork. Her eyes half closed as she enjoyed the first bite.

"I've never seen anyone do that before," he said, bringing his plate to the table.

She smiled as she cut through the stack for a second time. "My father always did this, except he covered the top with hot sauce. Everyone tells me eggs are bad for me, but I can't give them up. Whenever I have this breakfast, I feel close to him." She leaned right to nudge Daylon's shoulder. "Thanks, Daylon.

Truly."

He lifted a piece of bacon with his fingers. "I took care of Alice around the clock for the last year of her life," he murmured. "This is what I do." He said it in a matter-of-fact tone, but Haley felt his deep loss as a physical sensation. She looked into his eyes and felt a pain in her chest. He broke away from her gaze and crunched into his toast.

She went back to her story about the policeman who pulled her over. "I had a feeling that I knew that cop, but I couldn't see his face. He kept shining his flashlight in my eyes and the flashing lights from the patrol car pretty much blinded me."

"Do you know any cops in Canaburgh?" Daylon asked.

"I can't think of anyone in particular." She sipped the last of her coffee, and he got up to refill her cup. "The whole thing was totally weird. Who ever heard of a texting check?"

"I've heard of it," he said, "but not around here." He replaced the pot onto the coffeemaker and sat down. "Whenever something doesn't make sense, that's a sure sign some information is missing," he said, "or some fact you believe isn't actually true."

"As a counselor, I have a pretty thick skin," she said, "but this is getting to me."

"That's what he's counting on. If he wanted to hurt you, he would have done it first off. This is a fear campaign."

"Well, it's working."

He picked up her empty plate. "More coffee?"

"I need to get ready for work. Thanks for breakfast. This was just what I needed."

"I'll go over your car video today. I'll text you if I see something significant."

As she was leaving, Daylon said, "I can't put that tape on

118

your tail light while it's raining. When you get home, back the car up to the garage door, and I'll put it on then."

"Thanks again," she said and left. She had a full hour before she had to leave for work. Maybe she could set her alarm and nap for thirty minutes. She really needed it.

On the way to work, she thought about the two sources of a possible stalker: guys she had dated and clients. As far as clients go, she had about thirty appointments each week with an active caseload of about seventy people. Without something more to narrow down a search, she had no idea where to begin.

Suddenly she imagined Daylon's voice saying, "Begin at the beginning." That brought her back to Eli Loomis. Was there some way to contact other women who had dated Eli, to see if anyone else had trouble with him after a breakup? The dating site was no help, but Englewood and Canaburgh had fairly small populations. Someone must know something. People had patterns.

When she pulled into her parking space, she had another thought. She would ask Cheri for a reading.

Unfortunately, Cheri wasn't in the office that day.

When she reached home that afternoon, the rain had stopped. Daylon came to the garage door when she parked. He waved at her. "I'll take care of that tail light now," he said and disappeared inside.

She joined him. Wide work benches went along the left wall and part way across the back. A peg board hung above it with all kinds of tools and implements hanging from it. He dug around in a drawer and pulled out a roll of red tape.

"I've been thinking about Eli Loomis," she told him. "He has been single for seven years. I'm sure he has dated a lot of women who know how he reacts after a breakup."

Stooping down behind her car, Daylon nodded. "That makes sense." He ran a blue paper towel over the broken area.

Haley went on, "I was never at his house, but he said he lives somewhere between here and Canaburgh. He likes Rubio's restaurant and a couple other high-end places. I can list them. He also likes the movies, and there's only one movie theater in Canaburgh."

Daylon clipped off the strip of red tape and pressed it down. "I see what you're getting at. Someone on the waitstaff at those restaurants might know who he's been with." He applied a second strip.

"Or the movie theater. Maybe even some eating places here in Englewood." She paused. "Barb's staff might have seen him."

"Barb?"

"My best friend, Barb Morales. She owns the Cubana Cafe on State Street."

"Oh, yeah. They make great mac-and-cheese," he said, standing. "I go in there all the time."

She looked at him, surprised. "You know Barb?"

"Ever since I moved here," he said. "Let's go inside. I want to jot some notes before we lose this train of thought." He glanced at her blue dress pants and matching jacket. "I know. You have to go up and change."

"Why don't you bring your legal pad to my place in about twenty minutes?" she said. "I'll throw together some supper. You're always feeding me. Now it's my turn."

He grinned. "You've got a deal, young lady. You won't have to ask twice."

She took five minutes changing, then pulled containers out of her fridge. Leftover stir fry, a bit of cold chicken… She chopped an onion and put it into a large skillet with some olive oil. When Daylon knocked, she hurried to let him in. She didn't leave her door unlocked more than ten seconds, only whenever she slipped inside or out.

Hurrying back to her skillet, she added the vegetables and meat. "I'm throwing together a frittata," she said.

"A free-what?"

"Basically, you put all your leftovers into a pan and cover them up with egg and cheese."

"Smells great." He stopped at the door to slip off his loafers. "I went over your car video for the past week. Nothing. No one came near your car that I could see, and you didn't back into anything. If someone did that, they crawled in on their belly, out of camera range."

He took off his jacket and glanced around. "Your place is cozier than mine," he said, laying the jacket over the corner of her sofa. "I like what you've done with it." He set his legal pad on the table. "Can I pour drinks?"

"See what you like in the fridge," she said. "The glasses are in the same cabinet as yours."

He opened the fridge. "Ah!" he said, and pulled out a jug of iced tea. "You've got the good stuff."

Standing beside the stove, listening to him talk, Haley felt like they had known each other for years, like a friend from college or a distant cousin. How was that possible? She had known Daylon for a little over two months.

As they finished eating, he said, "We need a plan of action. How about if we look for restaurant staff who remember Eli and anyone he's dated."

"He made a scene with me," she said. "Maybe he made a scene with other women at these places."

"Better yet, maybe he dated someone they know. That would

be the jackpot."

"Don't forget the theater…" She hesitated. "Listen, Daylon." Her tone brought his attention away from his notes. "I can't let you do all this without payment. You're spending too much time and going to too much expense. I have to hire you."

His chin pulled back a little. "I told you I'm okay. We'll straighten it all out later. You've had a heavy financial hit, Haley, and it's not over yet."

She stood to gather their plates. "I feel like I'm taking advantage of your kindness. I have to hire you. I'm serious." She went to the sink.

"I'm serious, too," he said. "I don't want you as a client."

She turned around to face him, slightly offended. "Why not?"

He came out of his chair and pulled her into a dance pose. He lifted his hand so she turned. "That's why. I don't dance with my clients." He pulled her close. "I don't do this either." He kissed her firmly, then let her go.

She stared at him.

He watched her for a moment, more concerned with every passing second. "I'm sorry. I didn't mean to upset you."

She stepped into his arms and held on tight. He felt so right. He smelled so right. She couldn't let go. They stood in the kitchen, neither of them moving. Finally, Daylon pulled away.

"I like you, Daylon," she said. "I like you a lot."

"But…"

"But nothing. I'm exhausted from being up half the night scared out of my wits. This…" she waved her hand from him to her, "is too much for me right now. I need some sleep and some Valium, if I had any, which I don't." She sank down on her sofa and patted the seat next to her. "Let's sit here for a few minutes, okay?"

He sat beside her and put his arm around her. She lay her head on his shoulder. What a wonderful solid shoulder. It fit just right. She moved her head to settle in deeper, and breathed.

The next thing she knew, she woke up to see her kitchen clock at 2.10 a.m. She eased away from Daylon, who was sprawled across the sofa, sound asleep with his stockinged feet on the coffee table. She covered him with the pink throw and went to bed.

When she woke up to her alarm clock, she padded out to the living room in her bare feet. The throw lay piled in a heap. He was gone.

An hour later, Haley stepped outside on her way to work. Brilliant sunshine made her blink. She savored a deep breath of the warm morning air. Her sweater hung over her arm.

Daylon's door stood wide open, so she stepped closer, thinking she would call to him. Bees created a low hum around the masses of Stella de Oro edging his porch. He met her at the door, holding a blue hand towel.

He grinned at her. "First time I ever slept with a girl without getting lucky," he said. His chest jiggled with silent laughter, then he grew serious. "Last night, what I was trying to say in my bumbling screwup way was that we have to choose between personal and business. I wasn't going to go there just yet, but you didn't leave me much of a choice." He stepped closer. "I choose personal."

She moved in for a hug. "I slept better than I have in months, even with a crick in my neck."

He tightened his hold a little. "Me too. Be careful today, okay?"

She stepped back and gave his blue flannel shirt an

affectionate pat. "You can blame it all on this comfy shirt." With that, she set off for her car.

In a husky voice, he called after her, "I'll never take it off."

She called back. "Do you ever take it off anyway?"

"Ha!" He laughed and closed the door.

She started her car, and Creedence Clearwater Revival belted out "Have You Ever Seen the Rain?" For the first time in a long time, she sang along.

When she reached the office, Cheri was in the kitchen stirring her tea. "Well, well, well..." she said, looking Haley over. "You look rested."

"Thanks! I feel like last night was the first time I've really slept since March." She reached for the coffee pot. "Would you have time for a reading at lunchtime today?"

Watching her, Cheri nodded. "Sure. What's it about? Maybe I can pick up some information between now and then."

"I'm wondering if you can get a read on the stalker."

"Is he still bothering you?"

Haley told her about the tail light. "He's either someone I dated or a client." She stirred with a metal spoon clinking the side of the mug. "I can't seem to narrow down the possibilities. I was just wondering if you might be able to give me some ideas on what to look for."

Sipping from her mug, Cheri nodded. "Let's go out to your car at lunchtime. I might get something from the car."

"I appreciate it." She tasted her coffee and headed toward the hall.

Cheri called out before she reached the door, "You got laid!"

Haley laughed. She turned back and pointed at Cheri. "Nope. I did not get laid."

Frankie burst through the kitchen door like she was late.

"What? You got laid?" She stared at Haley's face, looking for clues.

Haley waved them both away. "I did not. That's the truth."

Cheri lifted her tea cup toward Haley. "There's a truth in there somewhere, girl. You can't lie to a psychic."

Haley quickly left the room. She knew a no-win situation when she saw one.

Chapter Eleven

Half an hour later, she was working on paperwork when she got a call on her business phone. A deep voice said, "This is Detective Banks. My partner and I took your statement regarding Flo Yeager, if you remember."

The bald guy named Banks. "Yes, I remember."

"We're bringing Fleeta Yeager to the police station for further questioning," he went on. "As a minor she has to have a sanctioned adult with her. Her father says he can't be there. He suggested we call you."

"I'm no longer her counselor," Haley said.

"You have a trusting relationship with the girl, so her father suggested you might be better than her new therapist. You're also nearby."

"If you're okay with it, I'm happy to sit with Fleeta." She pulled up her calendar. "When were you thinking?"

"This afternoon, if possible."

She scrolled through the day's appointments. "I'll move my last client. Will four thirty today work for you?"

"Thank you, Ms. Meyers. I'll leave instructions at the front desk." He ended the call.

Setting down the phone, Haley felt heaviness in her middle. The thought of Fleeta going through that traumatic story yet another time made Haley cringe. For the girl's sake, this needed to end soon.

Shortly after the detective called, Fleeta's father called. He sounded worried. "I'm in Philadelphia on business," he said. "The police just let me know they want to talk to Fleeta again. They offered to have a car pick her up and take her to the police station, but can you bring her home? She's liable to be upset, and I don't want her to ride home alone. My flight leaves here at one, so I should be at the apartment when she gets back."

Haley hesitated. This was highly unusual. "For Fleeta's sake, I'll say yes this time, although I don't usually drive clients in my car." She sighed. "I don't want to see her ride home alone either."

"I'll reimburse you for gas and time," he said and abruptly ended the call. What a sweetheart.

Haley glanced at the time and set her phone on airplane mode. This had turned into one of those non-stop days.

Joey arrived a few minutes later, looking refreshed and much calmer than the last time she had seen him. He wore a slightly wrinkled yellow polo shirt with a small green emblem on the chest. He seemed painfully thin without his bomber jacket. Was he losing weight?

He found a seat on her sofa, and Haley pulled up her notes. "How have you been, Joey?"

He adjusted the twill fabric on his pants legs, easing to a more comfortable position. "I'm still having nightmares, but they aren't as bad, and I know I'm dreaming, so I don't wake up freaked out like I used to."

"What about food? Are you eating?"

He shrugged. "I make myself meals, but I'm not all that hungry."

"But you are eating?" she asked.

He nodded. "I'm not starving myself if that's what you mean. Sometimes, I go to the diner and get a grilled cheese."

"What about anxiety…?"

"About a five. The meds are working."

"I'm glad to hear that. What about going out? Are you meeting up with friends or having people stop in to see you?"

He pushed up his glasses. He had deep circles under his eyes. "I haven't felt like going out. I've been in my workshop quite a bit and playing D&D. I've been in my troupe for almost six years now. So, I guess you could say I'm meeting up with friends, yes."

"D&D?"

"Dungeons and Dragons." He shifted to bring his right ankle up to his left knee, and clasped both hands on his shin. "I keep going over that day," he said. "I tried to write it all out, so I can get it out of my head—like you said—but—when I sit down to write, I start feeling all nervous and shaky."

"What makes you nervous?"

"It's about that guy...that guy I saw running across the yard. I keep thinking about that." He looked like he had just tasted something awful.

Haley waited for him to go on.

"I came upstairs to make myself a ham sandwich. I was looking out my kitchen window. I saw this guy in a black hoodie running across Flo's back yard. That was weird. It's the first time I ever saw someone come into her yard. I heard Fleeta screaming, so I ran over to help."

"You told the police this?"

Nodding, he went on, "He was built like a Dwarf Barbarian, short but heavy and strong. He ran pretty fast, too."

Making notes, she said, "What else was he wearing besides a hoodie?"

"Baggy black pants. He was kind of hunched over, like a linebacker with his shoulder forward."

"Shoes?"

"Some kind of boots, I think." He looked up, thinking. "Yeah, boots."

"I have an idea. How about if you write it out now? Do you think if I sit with you, you could do it? Maybe that would help you feel better. What do you think?"

He nodded, eager to please. "I'll try."

She stood up to find a fresh legal pad and pulled a pen from the black wire holder on her desk. "Write whatever comes to your mind. I'm not going to read it."

For the next twenty minutes, he wrote in precise block printing, filling three long yellow pages. Finally, he said, "I'm done," and set both the pen and tablet on the coffee table.

Haley tore off the pages and handed them to him. "Put them in your journal...or tear them up...burn them. Whatever feels best to you." He folded the papers and lay them beside him.

She glanced at the clock. "When did you become friends with Flo and Fleeta?" she asked.

"Flo was always kind to my mother," he said. "When Flo was going to the grocery store, she would take Mom with her sometimes, to give her an afternoon out." He sighed. "After Mom died, they took me in like I was part of their family."

His tone grew harsh. "Then Flo started dating Pauly. He treated me like I'm stupid. He didn't want me around. After a while, whenever he was there, I stayed away. When she broke up with him, they were fighting in the driveway. I kept watching out the window to make sure he didn't hurt her. I was ready to call the cops on him."

"Did he hurt her?"

He shook his head. "They shouted at each other. After a while, he put his arm up over his eyes, and he backed off. He got in his truck and left. Flo was crying really hard..." His voice trailed off. He stared at the wall as though reliving the scene.

Haley said, "Joey, you need to spend time with friends. Please, start going to your Steampunk Club again. Even if you don't feel like going out, it will be good for you."

He drew in a quivering breath and took off his glasses to wipe his eyes. He nodded and put his glasses back on.

"Do you want to take a minute before you go? You can sit here while I type my notes, if you like"

"I'm okay. Now that Fleeta's moved back into the house with her dad, things are better. Sometimes, we walk to the park." He jabbed at his glasses. "I'd like to go home now."

They made an appointment for the following week, and Joey left. Haley sat for a moment before filling out her paperwork.

Fleeta had moved back to Flo's house? She hadn't made an appointment. Strange.

Shortly before noon, Cheri stopped at Haley's open door. She had on her white muslin tunic with earrings made of peacock feathers and a long necklace of oddly shaped turquoise beads.

"Ready?" Cheri asked. She smiled smugly. "For someone who DIDN'T get laid, you certainly look good."

Not taking the bait, Haley closed her laptop. "Let's go."

The breeze was delicious. Gravel crunched under their shoes, and a vague hint of bright green hovered like a mist over the tree across the street—brand new leaves spreading out and reaching for the sun.

Cheri said, "I wish I had time to bring out a chair and soak up some of these rays." She made a slow circle around Haley's car, her hands up, palms outward, as though feeling the energy. At the rear of the car, she stopped and closed her eyes. "Someone was here. I'm feeling darkness, powerful anger…rage." She swallowed and took a small step back. "It's male energy, in charge, like he's a punisher. He's alone, and…" She took two steps back with her head turned to the side as though avoiding someone coming at her.

She stepped away for a second, then focused on Haley. "This guy is bad news. Please be careful. He could hurt someone. Don't let that someone be you."

"Did you get a name or description? Anything that would help me find him?"

She shook her head. "I wish I had." She shuddered. "*Whew!* I'm going to have to sage myself. This is freaking me out, Haley. Please be careful!" She set off for the building.

Haley stayed outside a few minutes longer. She wanted more time in the fresh air to clear her head. If only the weather could stay like this all year around.

Finally, she went inside. She didn't feel like eating lunch, so she made herself a cup of tea and went back to her office.

Joey had forgotten his journaled pages on the sofa. She picked them up and stuck them into his folder. When he came for his next appointment, she'd give them to him. She had insurance papers to fill out, and she'd better get busy.

Cheri's reading seemed disappointing, but she might have more come through later, after her emotions calmed down. In the movies, psychics tune in like opening a filing cabinet, and they find whatever information they want. That's not how it happened in the real world. When information did come through, it often appeared as impressions rather than concrete facts—a smell, an emotion or energy signature. The exception would be when connecting with departed spirits. A person on the other side can be very definite, but only when they want to be.

Before she left the office that afternoon, Haley noticed the door to Cheri's room stood open. She knocked on the door jamb and looked inside. Cheri was on her meditation cushion staring into space, her legs in lotus pose with her skirt pulled down over her knees. Suddenly, she looked at Haley, startled.

"Sorry," Haley said. "I didn't mean to disturb you."

Cheri smiled and shook her head. "I'm not meditating. I would have closed the door if I wanted privacy. I sat here to ground my energy. Come in."

Haley stepped further into the room. "Mind if I join you for about two minutes? I have to leave right away, but I wanted to check in with you before I go. I'm sorry the reading upset you."

Haley kicked off her kitten-heel pumps and sat cross-legged on the carpet. She closed her eyes and breathed in the scent of frankincense and patchouli.

A few seconds later, Cheri said, "You might want to write this down."

Haley grabbed her phone and typed herself an email as Cheri went on.

"I'm seeing a blue or light gray uniform shirt—like a security guard or something…He's squatting down behind your car. I'm behind him so I can't see his face." She opened her eyes. "If anything else comes through, I'll let you know."

Holding her phone, Haley slowly eased to her feet. "Thanks so much, Cheri. I'd hug you, but I can't bend down that far. I do have to run."

Sliding her phone into her purse, she hurried to her car and drove to the police station at the western end of State Street. As she turned off the car, she had a heavy feeling of dread. This wasn't going to be easy.

The small woman at the front desk led Haley to an interview room and closed the door. It was a small room with cinderblock walls painted light green. The only window was in the heavy metal door. It held a steel table big enough for six people but with only four chairs. Haley sat on the right side of the table, in the chair farthest from the door.

Within moments, Detective Banks came in holding a file. He wore a tired gray suit and white shirt, open at the neck. His jaw had a gray five-o'clock-shadow, and his mouth had weary lines on each side.

Still standing, he said, "Before they bring Fleeta in, I wanted a minute to speak with you. Some reports put the time of death at about an hour before the 911 call. What we're doing today is going back through the testimony of everyone involved to see if we can get more detailed information and set up a timeline. I'm going to press a little to see if we can pry loose any detail that might have been overlooked in Fleeta's previous statement, you understand?"

Haley nodded. "I'm not sure why you're telling me this."

"You can help us by keeping her calm and maybe helping her to remember. Just don't give her any information or ask her any questions. We're the ones doing the interview."

Haley nodded again. "I'll do my best. This is the first time I've been in this situation, so help me out if I cross a line, okay?"

"You'll do fine." He opened the door and the younger detective brought Fleeta in. She looked scared and immediately came to sit beside Haley.

Detective Banks sat across from Fleeta and smiled softly. "Hi, Fleeta," he said. "It's good to see you. We asked you to come in because we got some new information, and we need to check some things with you. This won't take long." He opened the folder and spoke a little louder. "For the record, we're recording this meeting, and I'm also taking handwritten notes."

He stated out the names of everyone present in the room, along with the date and time. "Before we get started on what

133

happened that day, let's go through this list of family and friends in the file."

He flipped pages in the file and found the right section. Calling out each name, he asked Fleeta to describe her mother's relationship with that person. All of Flo's family lived on the West Coast, so she rarely interacted with them. She got along with her neighbors. Fleeta couldn't think of a single enemy.

"What about school?" he said. "Did she have any problems with the mothers of your friends or your teachers?"

The most conflict Fleeta could recall was the time her mother made cookies for Fleeta's classroom and found out that they had to be purchased cookies delivered in an unopened package. Flo wasn't happy about that. Neither was the teacher. They ended up having an argument in the hall. That was when Fleeta was in second grade. She was currently in tenth.

Moving on, he said, "Okay, I'd like you to slowly give me everything you can remember on that day, from the time you got back to your house until the police arrived." Fleeta started to speak, but Detective Banks held up his hand. "We're going to take it super slow, like a movie in slow motion. I'll ask questions to help you, okay? Focus on the details, as many details as you can think of."

She nodded. Her silky black braid bounced against the collar of her jacket.

"What was the weather like that day?" For the next forty minutes, he carefully led her through her account, including a 360° view of her front yard. He did the same with the backyard, then leaned in. "Was anyone in the backyard?"

She thought carefully. "No. No one was around."

"Was anything out of place around the back door? On the sidewalk?"

"I saw my mom's car in the garage..." Pressing her lips together, she shook her head. "Everything was clean. Nothing

134

was there."

"What about the door? Was it unlocked?"

Her forehead scrunched. Closing her eyes, she lifted her hand, miming the motion. "I put the key in the deadbolt, but when I turned it, the lock felt loose. I tried the knob, and the door was unlocked."

"Did your mother usually leave the door unlocked?"

Emphatic, Fleeta shook her head. "She was really strict about locking it after we were inside. She had the locks changed when my dad moved out, but one time he walked right in because the door was left unlocked. Mom freaked out. After that, she wanted the doors locked all the time."

"Was she afraid of your father, Fleeta?"

"Not afraid... More like mad at him. She got so frustrated because he kept coming over and driving by our house." Her voice tensed. "She tried to tell him, but he wouldn't stop it."

Detective Banks made a note. "Did anyone else have a key to your house?"

"When we went on our trip, Mom gave Joey a key, so he could water the plants."

"And you were gone for how long?"

"Two weeks."

"So, you went inside..." He led her through a full description of everything she saw in the mudroom.

When the interview reached the stage of describing the kitchen, Fleeta wrapped her arms around herself. Her chin quivered. The younger detective left the room. He returned with a blanket and some water in a plastic cup. Haley helped him position the blanket around Fleeta's shoulders.

"Let's start with the kitchen, before you saw your mother on the floor."

"It was clean," she said. "It was really clean."

"Was it usually clean?"

135

Fleeta took a breath. "Mom wasn't a neat freak. When we left, breakfast dishes were in the sink. She didn't want to take the time to put them in the dishwasher. I poured cereal and spilled some on the counter. Stuff like that."

"And when you got back?"

"The whole place looked perfect." Her face crumpled. "Then I saw her." She leaned against Haley.

"Take your time," Detective Banks said. "Tell me the first thing that happened after you saw her."

Her breath came out in short gasps. "I tried to wake her up. When I couldn't, I started screaming. Joey ran over. When he couldn't wake her up either, he called 911."

"So, you screamed, and Joey came over. Do you have any idea how long it was from your first scream until Joey came over?"

Trembling, she hugged the blanket. "I screamed about three or four times. I can't remember how many."

"Did you have a sore throat after that?" he asked.

She swallowed. "A little. Not much."

"What did you do while you waited for the police to come?"

"I sat on the floor, crying. Joey sat next to me. When the police came, we moved out of the way and sat on the couch. Joey stayed with me until the woman came to take me to the group home."

When the interview was finally finished, Haley and Fleeta headed to the car. As depleted as Haley felt, she knew Fleeta had to need some time to debrief.

"Are you hungry?" Haley asked. "I think it might be good to stop and get something to eat. You'll feel better."

Tears welled up and spilled over. "I don't want to go back right now. Dad's going to ask me questions, and I can't answer any more questions right now."

Haley waited for her to buckle up, then put the car in gear

136

and headed for the diner. They both ordered noodle soup and a sandwich. Haley let the silence linger.

About halfway through her soup, Fleeta let out a deep sigh, and some of the tension eased out of her. She dropped a cracker into her bowl. "Dad's been great," she said. "He's always worrying about me." She nodded, as though assuring herself that he did worry. "He cried a lot about Mom. I think he was so mean because he was mad…about the divorce, I mean. But now he's great. I'm so glad to be with him instead of in that awful place."

Haley murmured, "I'm happy things are starting to work out for you."

She sighed again. "I'm really tired. Can we go home now?"

Haley signaled for the check.

Half an hour later, she walked with Fleeta to her door. Mr. Yeager yanked open the door and pulled his daughter into his arms. Over the girl's head he said to Haley, "Thank you for staying with her and bringing her home." He held out some folded bills.

Haley took the money. "You're welcome. I'm sorry for all you're going through. Bye, Fleeta." With a quick good night, she left them.

It was seven p.m. and fully dark. Tired to the bone, she saw Barb's car in her driveway and called her on the car's Bluetooth, sending out a silent plea that she would pick up. She did.

Haley said, "Hey, I'm driving home, and I'm tired. I thought maybe you could talk me in. Are you busy?"

Barb said, "I'm curled up on the sofa with a hot cup of tea. What's going on?"

"I just sat through a police interview on the Flo Yeager case."

Barb sounded worried. "They're interviewing you?"

"No, a minor who is a former client. She has to have an adult with her during questioning. That detective, Banks is his name, he's really good. I learned some things from him today. He got more information out of her than I would have ever thought possible."

"Care to share? Zoe's here. I'm putting you on speakerphone."

"Hi, Haley!" Zoe called out. She sounded much younger than she was. Both Barb and Zoe were thirty eight years old, born six days apart. Barb was older, and Zoe would not let her forget it.

"She's not a client," Haley said, "so I can tell you about it. The most important thing was that the house was clean, like spotless. Flo was more of a messy housekeeper, not worried about every speck and crumb. They had gone on vacation with stuff in the sink and things lying around. When they came back, everything was...clean."

Barb said, "So, someone broke in and cleaned the house...but didn't take anything?"

Zoe yelled. "Maybe they'll hit us next!" She squealed, then giggled. "Cut it out, Barb!"

Haley laughed. "You guys are a hoot. Thanks for sticking with me. I'm home now. Talk to you later. Love you! Bye!"

Daylon's parking space was empty. Haley slipped into comfy clothes and found a cold chicken breast in the fridge. She made herself a sandwich and a wine spritzer, then sat at the table. Taking a bite of her sandwich, she turned to a clean page on the legal pad and drew four columns. She labeled them Name, Means, Motive and Opportunity.

Chapter Twelve

In the left column, Haley wrote *Pauly Hammond*. He had a motive, for sure. Flo had recently told him their relationship was over for good.

Haley tapped the pen, thinking. Would Flo turn off her security system and open the door for Pauly? Maybe. She had taken him back before. If she had let him in, and they had a fight, things could have become ugly fast. He had three out of three. She circled his name.

How about Flo's ex-husband? Haley always called him Mr. Yeager because she couldn't remember his first name. Flo had always called him "my ex." Now that Flo was gone, Fleeta automatically went to live with him. That was a motive. Someone had seen him cruising the neighborhood that day, so he had an opportunity. Means was a given. She circled his name.

She wrote Black Hoodie next. That guy was still a complete mystery. Even now, no one had a clue about his identity. He had means and opportunity, but until they found out who he was, he was a dead end: motive unknown.

Leaving the tablet on the table, she moved to the sofa and stretched out. She adjusted the fuzzy throw over her legs, idly scanning YouTube on her phone, feeling soft and sleepy. She must have dozed off because a few minutes past nine, a text from Daylon jolted her awake. A box on her screen said: You still up?

Haley: Yes

Daylon: Okay if I come up?

Haley: Yes

Seconds later, he tapped on her door. She pulled it open, and said, "Good timing. I'm going over some things, and I was wishing you were here."

He moved inside, gazing into her eyes in a purposeful way. "That the only reason?"

Her heart lurched.

He reached for her, and she went to him willingly. "I've been waiting for this all day," he murmured. Crushing her to him, he kissed her like a thirsty man.

Haley's head spun. She clung to him as her knees gave out. When they paused to take a breath, she murmured into his ear, "I was wondering when you would get around to that."

He rubbed his cheek against her hair. "I didn't trust myself to kiss you again. I knew if I did…" He eased his face around her cheek to find her lips again...and the world went away.

Hours later, Haley blinked and made out a circle of light around the edge of her bedroom curtains. The alarm clock showed 5.23. She let out a contented sigh and eased closer to Daylon. Not wanting to wake him, she rested her head against the top of his arm.

Without opening his eyes, he lifted his arm, and she slid her head onto his chest as naturally as if they had been together for years. The next Haley knew, her seven thirty alarm was buzzing.

"I have to work today," she mumbled. Her mouth tasted like sawdust.

He glanced at the clock. "I'm a lazy bum. I'm usually up by five thirty." He hugged her tight, then released. "OK, I'll let you go." He kissed her hair where it brushed his jaw.

Feeling dazed, she got up and headed toward the shower. She stood for a long moment with the hot spray blasting into her face.

140

She had to pull herself together. She had six clients today.

"Coffee?" Daylon called to her.

"Yes," she yelled back. "I feel hungover."

He replied, "I'm going to my place. I'll have coffee and breakfast for you when you come down."

Haley turned the heat up on the water, easing her muscles under the pressure. She let it course down her spine for a few more minutes. She could definitely get used to this.

She dressed in white capris with a yellow shirt and white linen overshirt. She'd have to throw on a big sweater, but she didn't care. She wanted to dress like spring.

On her way downstairs, she picked up the legal pad she had been working on the night before. When she came in, Daylon was pouring coffee into mugs at his table. He set her plate of pancakes and eggs onto the table and picked up the pad. Scanning it, he said, "I thought you weren't going to get involved in the police investigation."

She shrugged. "Yesterday, I attended Fleeta's third police interview as her adult sponsor. That got me thinking about the murder again. I wrote down those notes when I got home, not that I'm going to do anything with them."

He picked up his plate and joined her at the table. "What you have written there is good," he said, "but you have some gaps."

"Like what?" She took a bite. "Mmmm...these pancakes are perfect."

He leaned over for a quick kiss. "You listed the people who have been obvious from the start. What about people who aren't so obvious? Who were the first people to find her? Who was the last person to speak to her? That kind of thing."

"You think Fleeta is a suspect? That's not feasible."

He set the pad down and picked up his fork. "If you're going to play detective, you'll have to think like an investigator. No one is off the table until they have definitely been cleared by an alibi or lack of means or standing to lose from their death. People do crazy things sometimes. They leave things out of their statements and get the facts mixed up. It takes some digging to find out what's actually going on."

Haley chuckled. "That sounds like what I deal with every single day in my sessions." Draining her coffee cup, she stood. "I'll leave that pad with you. My day is jammed, so I won't be able to look at it until later anyway."

He stood for a quick hug good-bye. When he squeezed her tight, he made a humming noise that sounded something like *MMMMM-mmmm.*

At her office, Haley kept her door closed and stayed inside all day, except for a couple of quick restroom breaks. The last thing she wanted was to run into Cheri or Frankie and hear their teasing. Haley wanted this tender feeling all to herself, at least for a while.

She spent her lunch break going through her patient folders, looking for anyone—client or family member—who might stalk her as revenge for some imagined wrong. She came up with three people within the past four months. Now that she was working systematically, she felt stupid for not doing this sooner. She had been too obsessed with Pauly Hammond.

Just to cover all the bases, she put Pauly on the list, so she could eliminate him. He had three out of three for most of the stalking events, but Daylon had seen him in the hospital for the last one. Instead of eliminating him, she put a question mark in the Opportunity column.

Jovan Jansen had sued her in January. He was pretty worked up, that's for sure, so yes to Motive and Means. But he had taken a job and moved away from Englewood. That put him out of reach. Another question mark for Opportunity.

In early February, she had released a teenager with an addiction because he had lied to her. She couldn't work with someone who wasn't motivated to do the work. He seemed more relieved than upset when she let him go, but she wrote his name anyway. She drew a big question mark under motive for him.

Who else? She picked up her phone and called Barb. "Got a minute?" she asked.

"Sure. I'm not working today. What's up?"

Haley told her about the list she was putting together. "I've gone through my client list and came up with three names, but none of them pop. Can you think of anyone else who might be really mad at me?"

Barb laughed. "Well, you outed Linda's husband, as I recall."

"Oh my God. You are right." She wrote his name on the page. "You think Mr. Smiley Face would dirty his hands to get back at me? He might ruin his manicure."

"Well, he might hire someone else to do it," Barb said. Suddenly, she burst out, "Love you, *mija,* but I've got another call." She clicked off.

Looking over the list, Haley felt pain on every line of that chart. No wonder her practice drained her so much. Broken relationships, love gone wrong, betrayal...so much anguish. She sat with these stories every day. What most people called love was actually control, manipulation and even obsession.

Where did that leave her? Was she delusional to think about a new relationship? What had developed with Daylon came at her sideways, a casual acquaintance that took a sudden right turn. Or maybe that was a left turn. Whatever it was, she was going to let it play out and see what happened. She had never been with a man who was as easy to be around as Daylon Jasper. She had dated several men who made her feel safe, but Daylon went beyond safe. He felt like home.

When she got back to the apartment that afternoon, Daylon was working on something in the garage. She waved to him and went upstairs. Inside her apartment, she dropped her purse, kicked off her shoes and headed for the bedroom to lie down. She was completely and totally exhausted.

She woke up after eight, starving. Her phone was still in her purse. When she pulled it out of the side pocket, she had a text from Daylon from three hours ago: How about some Chinese takeout?

She texted back: Sorry. I fell asleep.

Daylon: I figured. Let's catch up tomorrow, okay?

Haley: I'm sleeping in until at least ten. I've been tired all day, thanks to you. You have a lot of energy for an old guy. LOL

Daylon: <winky face> Sleep tight.

Smiling softly, she made herself a sandwich and headed back to bed, basking in the sheer luxury of time without an alarm clock.

Shortly before noon, Daylon tapped on her door. "Hey, sleepyhead," he said when she opened it. He came in for a long hug. "I've been working on something. Want to see it?" He held up a pad filled with ink.

Locking the door behind him, she sat next to him on the sofa. He showed her the pages. "I made a chart for your stalker."

She laughed and shook her head at him. "You didn't!" Reaching for her purse, she found a folded page and handed it to him. "Yesterday, I went through all my patient files for the past two years. All four hundred of them."

Opening the paper, he sang, "You and me, girl. We've got something going on."

She smiled. "You have that on a CD?"

He nodded. "'Islands in the Stream.' Sure, I do." He grew serious and put the paper down. "You should have an actual security system hooked up, one that calls the police when the alarm is tripped."

She felt tension in her face and sighed. "I need to accept the fact that he's not going to get tired and stop on his own." She tilted her head to look at him next to her. "That's what I should have done at the very beginning, isn't it? I've fumbled around and made a mess. I feel so stupid, Daylon. I should know better."

He put his arm around her. "Listen. You had no idea what was going to happen. Stop blaming yourself. You're not the one causing the problem."

"It's hard for me to accept that someone would go this far." She paused. "I tell people things they don't want to hear. If I didn't, I wouldn't be doing my job. Sometimes they get mad but never like this."

"Tell me about the people on the list," he said, "the ones I don't already know."

When she got to Linda's husband, Daylon's eyebrows raised. "You did what?"

"I told her… Well, I showed her his face in the dating app. No explanation was required."

He scratched his hair above his temple. "You're telling me that he put himself out there on a dating app in the same town where his wife knows most of the population? Who would do that?"

"When you put it that way, it's pretty insane, isn't it? To be fair, he probably listed his town as some distance away but the range included Englewood. The range is what got him."

"If you say so. I've never been on a dating site in my life."

"Have you dated much since Alice passed?" she asked.

He glanced at her. "You are the first and only."

She gave him a wide-eyed stare. "You were so flirty with me. I thought you were on the prowl. You know, a player."

He smirked, in a self-deprecating gesture. "It took me years to finally work myself up to flirting. I hadn't gotten to actually dating yet. Alice and I were together since we were in high school. I haven't dated in…"

"Let me guess… more than thirty years?"

He looked surprised.

"It was more than twenty years for me. There are a lot of us out there, Daylon. Newly single and trying to figure it out at our age. What a time we live in."

"You've been single for how long?" he asked.

"Four years. But my situation was different. Bob was distant and cold. He wasn't interested in knowing his own children, and least of all me. When our youngest left, I did, too. I needed more from life than what was left in that empty house." She sighed. "I've tried dating a few different times and had a couple of relationships, but nothing serious. Last fall, I figured I'd try one more time." She leaned her head back and groaned. "Look where it got me."

He took her hand. "I have an idea. How about if we go to an early movie, followed by dinner at Rubio's?"

"Rubio's? How can I resist an offer like that?"

He hesitated. "I don't like the idea of taking you out on a date in my old pickup truck. Would you mind if we take your car?"

"As long as you're driving."

An hour later, they were on their way with Hall and Oates on the stereo.

Daylon said, "We can ask some questions while we're there. Do you have a photo of Eli on your phone?"

She frowned and shook her head. "I'm not much of a selfie person. Let me see…" She scrolled through her photos and ended up shaking her head. "Nope. That's what I thought…Wait a minute. Maybe if I go back to the app, I can find him and take a screenshot." Thirty seconds later, she had it. "I've been meaning to uninstall this from my phone. Do you think I should leave it on here a while longer in case we need information?"

He gave her a sly grin. "I have to admit I have mixed emotions on that one."

She laughed. "You know the definition of mixed emotions? Watching your mother-in-law go over a cliff…"

"…in your brand-new Cadillac," he finished with her. His chest jiggled with silent laughter. "I went to grade school, too. That one was number one on the charts in third grade, as I recall."

She nudged his arm. "Smartypants." She reached for the center console and slid a fresh CD into the player. Air Supply filled the car with "Making Love Out of Nothing at All."

He reached over and held her hand for the rest of the trip.

Located on the end of a small strip mall, the Canaburgh movie theater was built in the 1980s with green indoor/outdoor carpet and push-button water fountains. It was clean, but it needed an upgrade. As they slowly wound their way inside, Daylon showed Eli's photo to a few people, but he got no hits.

With one popcorn bucket to share and two water bottles, they settled into the back row of an action-comedy movie. Always quick to laugh, Haley was in tears over a scene where the hero posed as a mural painter as a cover for surveillance. She was six

147

feet off the ground on simple scaffolding with a row of open paint cans lined up on the shelf beside her. A dufus carrying a ladder swung around and the paint cans went flying. The gag was ancient, and Haley had seen it performed a hundred different ways. Still, she went into a laughing spasm and ended up knocking over the popcorn bucket. Daylon rescued it with a little still left inside.

He looked at her, his chest jiggling.

She gasped and covered her mouth to keep from making noise, tears streaming down her cheeks.

He grinned and picked up a piece of popcorn. "Who needs a movie?"

She pushed him on the shoulder.

When people started leaving during the final credits, Daylon and Haley stayed in their seats. They had a whole hour until their restaurant reservation, so they might as well wait until the crowd left.

"I don't know why that was so funny," she said. "It was idiotic." Despite her words, she giggled. "I'm a sucker for slapstick. What can I say?" Suddenly, she grabbed Daylon's arm. "That's him!" she whispered.

He glanced at her and tried to follow her line of sight. "Who?"

"Eli Loomis. He's with that woman in the red shirt, third row from the bottom."

"Stay here until the place clears out," Daylon said, "then wait for me in the lobby. I'm going to get his license plate number." He slid out of his seat and made his way down the wide steps. Moving casually but purposefully he positioned himself a few feet behind Eli and his date.

Haley watched them until they disappeared around the

corner. Her heart was jumping. In such a small town, it wasn't surprising that they had run into Eli. But what if he was also going to Rubio's?

Ten minutes later, Daylon came through the lobby doors. "I got it," he said. "Let's wait here a few minutes until they pull out."

"What if they go to Rubio's?" she said.

"Let's hope not. It wouldn't be good for me to waltz in there with you after I just shadowed them out to the parking lot. He definitely saw me." He looked around. "I'm going to duck into the men's room while we're waiting."

A few minutes later, they left the theater. When they pulled into Rubio's parking lot, Eli's car was nowhere in sight.

Inside, the hostess gave Daylon a friendly smile. He said, "Hi, Sally. Looks like a busy evening."

"Daylon," she said, showing perfect teeth. "How are you?" She was about Frankie's age with a heart tattoo under her left ear.

"I'm great. This is Haley." He turned to Haley. "I helped Sally's mother with a problem a couple of years ago." He showed the picture of Eli to the girl. "Do you know him?"

She nodded. "Comes in all the time. I'm not a fan. No one here is."

"Do you know any of his regular dates? It's for a case I'm working on."

"You mean women he's brought in here?" She thought for a moment, then nodded. "I believe he was dating Eunice's mom for a while. Eunice is a dishwasher." A family came in, so she said, "I'll show you to your table," and led them toward the back of the dining room.

Decorated in burgundy and dark wood, the room had three rows of square wooden tables turned at an angle to allow some privacy. Each held a flickering candle in a low bowl and gold cloth napkins rolled up with silverware inside.

Daylon seated Haley, then sat in the chair next to her.

Sally took their drink orders. Before she left, she said, "I'll get that information for you in a few minutes," and hurried away.

Haley said, "I'm impressed. You know a lot of people around here."

He leaned in, almost touching shoulders with her. "You get a lot further if people feel comfortable around you. I call it relationship equity. Not just for the P.I. stuff, but in life, don't you think?"

"I can see that."

"When I was in the Corps, relationships were all we had. My first CO taught me that a soft manner and quiet words go a lot further in the long run. I've never forgotten that."

Their server appeared with their teas, and they ordered.

When the girl left, Haley asked, "How long were you in?"

"Twenty-five years. I was in Afghanistan shortly after 9/11 and went back a second time in 2004. I finally retired in 2009. After that, I worked in private security for a couple of years and got my P.I. license."

"You're so laid back. I expected you to be more..." she searched for a tactful word, "...bossy."

He lifted his chin, watching her. "Oh, so that's why you gave me the cold shoulder when you first moved in?"

At that moment their food arrived, and Haley was glad to change the subject. She twirled her fork in the fettuccini and took that amazing first bite.

"I wish I knew how they season this," she said. "Whoever made the recipe was a genius."

Diving in for a mussel, Daylon nodded. "It's magic. And it's always the same."

They didn't speak again for a while. When Haley put down her fork, she realized that their plates were pushed toward each other. They were both leaning into the corner of the table, casually enjoying the food and bringing up the best parts of that night's movie from time to time.

When they couldn't hold another bite, they asked for takeout boxes. Haley pressed her hands over her stomach. "So good. Thank you for bringing me here."

He grinned. "The pleasure, as they say, is all mine."

Sally dropped off a folded note as she passed their table. Daylon opened it and showed Haley a phone number in blue ink. "I'll call that tomorrow." He gave her a pleased smile. "Now we're getting somewhere."

When they arrived home, it was still daylight. Daylon followed her upstairs. Melting into his arms, Haley let the powerful magnetic surge sweep her along. She was falling for this guy. She couldn't stop it. She didn't want to.

Chapter Thirteen

The next morning, Daylon rolled over, bringing Haley partially awake. He kissed her cheek and murmured, "I'm going for a run. Get some good sleep." She drifted off and didn't wake up again until ten fifteen.

She was just out of the shower when Daylon knocked on her door. The moment she heard the sound, she knew something was wrong. Hair dripping, she threw on a robe and peeked outside.

He said, "You've got a brick through the back window of your car. You'd better come down."

Her shoulders sagged. "I'll get dressed."

"Take your time. It's not going anywhere."

She spent a few minutes blow drying her hair. Pulling on jeans and a shirt, she looked for her sneakers. Her poor car. *How much was all this going to cost?*

Holding her phone with the video app ready, she stepped outside to see Daylon at the end of the driveway, talking to a woman in a blue jogging suit. The woman handed Daylon something, then ran down the sidewalk past a teenage boy walking a yappy dachshund.

Glass sparkled on the black macadam driveway, and Haley started recording video on her phone. When she saw the damage to her window, she let out a groan. A giant red brick hung in the wires that defrost the back window. The glass had a web of fractures with a corner of the brick punching a hole through the center of the web.

"Why didn't my car alarm go off?" she said. She stopped the video to send a text. Speaking into the phone, she texted Sgt. Kirk, "This is Haley Meyers. He threw a brick through the car window." Autocorrect entered: *He threw off Rick through the car window.* Scowling, she typed the correction.

Kirk texted back: I'm ten minutes out. Are you safe?

Haley: Yes

Just then, a text came in from the stalker's blocked number: *We're just getting started. I can keep this up forever.*

Haley scoffed and muttered, "Whatever." She was over it.

Joining her near the back corner of the car, Daylon said, "I saw the damage when I came out this morning. Instead of going for a run, I went house to house down this entire street and asked people for last night's security footage of any street-facing cameras. Someone just dropped off a thumb drive. I'll have more of them in a little while." He rubbed his stubbled jaw. "Unfortunately, your footage from the car camera only shows a shadow. Totally worthless, except for the timestamp. At least we know it happened around four a.m."

"You saw this hours ago?"

He turned to her. "I'll be damned if he was going to interrupt your sleep again and have you start the day all upset. What's the difference anyway?"

She shrugged. "You're absolutely right. I just texted the policeman, but a lot of good he's going to do. I can tell that you already." She showed him the stalker's text. "Believe it or not, I'm not mad or scared right now. I'm disgusted. Totally disgusted."

"We've got to get your car out of the driveway. I'll clear out the right bay of the garage, so you can pull your car inside from now on."

She moved closer to get a better look at the damage. "Most car insurance covers glass," she said. "I'll give them a call."

Sgt. Kirk arrived and parked nearby. He took pictures with his phone. Pulling out his notepad, he asked a few questions and wrote down the details. A few minutes later, he left.

His lack of solutions only added to Haley's frustration. She thought the police were supposed to protect and serve. She certainly didn't feel protected and definitely not served.

Daylon went into the garage for a push broom to clear the driveway of glass. Haley was vacuuming the back seat when the glass repair truck arrived. Filling out the insurance paperwork took almost as long as the repair. Less than an hour later, she had a new window.

Shortly after noon, she eased her car inside the garage. By that time, Daylon had six thumb drives in the buttoned pocket of his blue flannel shirt. When she joined him near the open garage door, he put his hands on her shoulders, his face tilted down toward hers. "How are you?"

"I've been better." She rested her cheek against the place where his neck met his shoulder, letting his presence stabilize her rocked emotions. In a moment, she said, "Want to nuke the leftovers from Rubio's for lunch?"

He nodded. "I'll bring up my laptop, so we can look at these thumb drives. Maybe you'll recognize someone." He pulled down the garage door, and the lock clicked.

Upstairs, Haley scraped the mussels and clams out of their shells and poured the pasta into a saucepan. This meal was far too delicate and delicious for a microwave.

When Daylon tapped on her door, she hurried to let him in. She felt paranoid, and she hated feeling paranoid. When patients exhibited these behaviors, she would recommend them to a

154

psychiatrist for medication. Come to think of it, maybe she should make an appointment herself. She had a feeling that her blood pressure wasn't doing too great right now.

When he came in, she eyed Daylon's laptop. "Would you mind if we look at the footage after we eat?" she asked. "I'm getting pretty tired of eating meals focused on that jerk."

He set the laptop on the coffee table and joined her in the kitchen. "That smells great."

"I know. I can't wait! As often as I eat this dish, I never get tired of it." She brought their plates to the table. "It sounds weird, but I feel like I've been approaching this whole stalker thing backwards. I don't know how to explain it, but I keep thinking that if I had started out with the attitude and determination that I have now, things would have wrapped up so much sooner. You know what I mean?"

He scratched the back of his hair and smoothed it down. "Like what?" He took a seat.

"Well, if I had installed a top-notch security system from the beginning—both car and house—parked my car in the garage and checked the neighbors for security footage, that guy would already be behind bars. I would have saved so much in so many ways. Not to mention the sleep I've lost and my blood pressure." She sat next to him at the table.

"You're learning," he said. He kissed her cheek. "Let's enjoy this great lunch, okay?"

She leaned sideways to press his shoulder for a second, then picked up her fork. "How is Scott's rehab going?" she asked. "You haven't mentioned him lately."

Daylon chuckled. "He's a bad patient. Too much like his old man, I'm afraid."

Half an hour later, they snuggled on the sofa with Daylon's

laptop between them. While it loaded the application, Daylon said, "We're looking for a car or someone walking down the street around four a.m."

"Thank God for street lights," she said.

A few minutes later, the video showed someone passing through a pool of light across the street from the camera. He wore a black hoodie and black pants. Even with the camera focused right on him, he was a sauntering shadow.

Daylon muttered something under his breath. "Cameras aren't going to do it for us, Haley. He knows how to get around them. He's probably wearing a black mask, too. That's why the car camera didn't catch him." He put his palms together and tapped his mouth, thinking. "A stakeout. It has to be a stakeout with the cops on speed dial."

"You'd miss a lot of sleep. He might not be back for weeks. Now that the car's hidden away, he might not be back at all." She peered at the frozen image on the screen. "Let me see him walk again. I might recognize the body language." She watched the video several times. "I know I've seen that person before, but I have no idea who it is."

She paused to peer at the still image. "See where his head reaches on the light pole? That could be Eli Loomis, but I can't see Eli going all ninja like that. He's too macho to hide."

Daylon said, "I'm going to talk to a friend of mine who's a P.I. I need a fresh pair of eyes. Maybe I'm missing something." He closed the laptop and set it on the coffee table. "Now that we're treating this like a series of crimes, like a rash of neighborhood break ins, we're going to get him. Maybe not tomorrow, but we will get him. I finally feel like we're getting ahead of this."

Suddenly, he looked startled. "Hey, I almost forgot. Sally

gave me Eunice's phone number." He pulled the slip of paper from his jeans pocket, punched the number into his phone and put it on speaker.

While it rang, Haley said, "Well, that's one benefit of wearing the same clothes all the time."

He smirked and touched her side with his elbow.

A soft girl's voice answered, "Hello?"

"Hello, Eunice? We were at Rubio's last night, and Sally said you might be able to help us. My name is Daylon. I'm here with Haley."

Silence.

"We're looking for someone who can give us some information about a man named Eli Loomis."

"What did he do?" she asked.

Haley spoke up. "Maybe nothing. I dated Eli from SeniorsMatch.com, and I'm looking for other women who also dated him."

"My mom dated him last year," Eunice said. "She's here. Do you want to talk to her?"

"That would be great," Haley said, relief in her voice.

A moment later, a suspicious woman said, "Who is this?"

"My name is Haley Meyers. I dated Eli Loomis up until a few weeks ago. Someone is stalking me, and I don't know who it is. I'm trying to find other women Eli dated to see if he might act this way after a break up. Can you please help me?"

The woman's voice relaxed a little. "I'm Angela. I dated Eli for ten months. We were actually talking about marriage. After a while he got too controlling, and I had to break up with him. He slashed my tires a couple days later."

"Are you sure it was him?"

"Yeah. He left his pocket knife in one of the tires. It was him

157

all right."

"Angela, I'm not one hundred percent sure Eli is the one doing this to me," Haley said. "Is it okay if I call you back if I need more help?"

"Sure." She gave Haley her cell number, then said, "I never called the police. I was too afraid of what he might do if I turned him in. You're braver than I was. Nail him!" She got off the call.

Daylon's eyes widened in mock surprise. "Wow. Don't get on her bad side."

She smirked. "Did you hear her? She's all bark and no bite." Haley snagged her list of potential stalkers from the coffee table. "Now that we know he's a big guy, we can cross the shorter men off the list, like Mr. Yeager." Haley drew a line through his name. "Same for my teenage client... and, believe it or not, Pauly Hammond."

Daylon nodded. "He's way too short. What about Linda's husband?"

Haley considered. "We can't rule him out. By the way, his name is Scott Blankenship."

"I won't forget that. My son's name is Scott."

A few minutes later, Daylon left to run some errands and visit his son. Haley cleared away the lunch dishes. She pulled out a good book and stretched out on the couch to read and nap and read and nap until the light grew too dim to read any more.

When she turned on the brass lamp near her head, Dad was sitting in the lounge chair.

"Hi," she said. "It's good to see you."

He beamed at her. "I've waited a long time to hear you say that."

"How's Linda?"

"She's doing well. She doesn't think so, but she is."

"I've been meaning to ask you something," Haley said.

"Anything."

"Where's Mom?" Her mother had passed ten years ago.

"She was with you and your sister until I crossed," he said. "A couple of years ago, she decided she wanted to come back in." He tilted his head as though listening. "She's due for re-entry in... two more months." He chuckled. "She's so cute as a little kid. I'm looking forward to seeing her. When she goes in, I'll watch over her, the same as I do you. We've done this more times than I can count."

"Speaking of watching over...," Haley said, "do you have any idea who might be stalking me? Have you found any new information?" She held up her phone to show him the video.

"I looked into your record, and he's not going to harm you, Haley. You're going to catch him before much longer. That's as much as I can tell you now. I'm sorry, honey."

"I just want it to be over," she said. "My nerves are on edge all the time."

He sent her a wave of warmth as he faded out. "Life is about the journey, Haley. The journey."

Yeah, yeah, yeah, she replied in her mind as she opened her book. *I'm pretty worn out with this particular journey.*

On Wednesday, Haley arrived at the Healing Circle a few minutes early. Sonia spotted her coming through the door and hustled her into the bookstore office, a room half the size of Haley's apartment kitchen.

Watching Sonia close the door behind them, Haley said, "What's going on?" She had never seen Sonia close that door before.

Keeping her voice low, Sonia said, "Daylon was here this morning. He was grinning like the cat that swallowed the canary.

I swear, he looks at least ten years younger." She beamed at Haley, thrilled to the core. "I finally got it out of him that you're seeing each other."

Haley let out a gasp. "I never figured him to kiss and tell," she said, smiling widely in spite of herself.

Sonia hugged her. She was as tiny as a child. "He's been sad and quiet for so long, Haley. I've been worried about him." She practically danced with delight. "Something told me you would hit it off."

"Wait a minute... Is that why you offered me the apartment? Did you set me up?"

She cleared her throat. "Let's just say, I was hoping things would work out. You never know till you try, right?" Her eyes sparkled.

Haley watched her. "I guess not."

"He's a good man, Haley. He was so good to my sister. No one could have done more." She finally took a breath. "All kidding aside, I hope it works out for both your sakes because I feel the same way about you." She reached for the door knob. "We'd better get to the meeting." As Haley passed by her, Sonia pinched the sleeve of Haley's jacket and gave it a happy little shake.

Martin was in the hallway when they came out. Shiny bald on top, he had a longish gray fringe around the sides of his head. He briefly made eye contact with Haley, a smile behind his gaze. The news was out, that's for sure.

Everyone was present today, and they had a lot to share. Barb had a tray of finger sandwiches, along with a crockpot of vegetable soup and some wide mugs stacked on the counter.

Haley arrived at the counter as Frankie was filling her soup mug.

160

"Haley!" Frankie said, glancing up. "I have something for you in my office. It's been there since last week. For some reason, I keep missing you."

"What is it?" Haley asked, picking up a ham-and-cheese sandwich.

"It's a surprise!" She hurried away before Haley could say more.

Cheri started the meeting before Haley sat down. "We have a lot of catching up to do, so let's get started while we eat—and many thanks to Barb for bringing lunch! Who wants to be first to share?"

Linda said, "I will. As you know, I had the crazy idea that catching Scott red handed on that dating site would make the divorce go through without a hitch. My lawyer just got word from his lawyer that Scott is claiming someone used his picture on the dating sites. It was identity theft and not him at all."

"It was him," Cheri said.

Frankie chimed in. "That's what I'm getting, too, Cheri."

Linda's green eyes flashed. "I know it was him! But I have to get proof. I'm going to find a private investigator and build a case."

Sonia chimed in, "Haley knows a good one. Ask her."

All eyes went to Haley.

"What are you talking about?" she said, suddenly uncomfortable.

Cheri said, "Oh, so you did get laid. Are you still denying it?"

Haley gasped, laughing. "I'm a grown woman. What is the big deal?"

Frankie said, "Sonia, you know something, don't you? We tried to get it out of her last week, but she's not telling."

Haley said, "I'm seeing Sonia's brother-in-law, Daylon Jasper…" She glanced at Linda, "…who happens to be a private investigator."

"And a good one," Sonia added.

Linda said, "One of you, text me his number?"

Sonia pulled out her phone. "I'll do it now."

Cheri arched her eyebrows, gazing at Haley. "Okay, Haley. Your turn."

Haley laughed. She wasn't the least bit embarrassed, but her cheeks burned. "Daylon has been helping me with the stalker situation. Which means we've been spending quite a bit of time together. End of story." She glanced at Cheri. "Oh, and by the way, I was telling the truth when you thought you outed me."

Sharing a knowing glance with Frankie, Cheri said, "So that was a prediction, huh?"

Trying to swallow a smile that wouldn't take no for an answer, Haley pulled out her phone. "I have something to show you guys. It's a video of the stalker… not that you can see much. He's wearing black, and it's at night." She handed the phone to Barb, next to her. "Does anyone recognize his walk or anything about him that might give us an idea of who he is? He threw a brick through my car window on Sunday night."

Horrified, Barb gasped, "*Dios mio!* Haley, you have to come to stay with us. He could hurt you." Barb stared at the movement on the screen. Linda leaned over Barb's shoulder to watch.

Haley said, "I have lots of cameras set up all over the place, but as you can tell, they aren't doing much good. Even with a camera right on him, we can't tell who it is. Another thing, I have to get connected to a security company, so the police will get a call—in case he decides to break into my apartment."

Barb's eyes grew round. "You can't stay there!" she said.

"We have to catch him," Haley told her. "I can't keep running away. He has to be stopped."

Frankie said, "Conley works for a security company. They're local."

"We use that company," Cheri said. "They've been good." She took the phone from Linda and watched the video. "I know that guy," she said. She closed her eyes, squinting a little with concentration. "Who is he? Who is he?" Suddenly, she looked at Haley. "I can see him in the...waiting room?" She squeezed her eyes closed. "I've definitely seen him in the building."

"At Alexion?" Haley said.

Cheri nodded. "He has been in the building."

Barb said, "Can you get more about what he looks like, Cheri?"

Cheri closed her eyes, intent. "He's a big guy. Not muscles though. Big and soft." She breathed in long and slow. "His face is round with puffy cheeks. White guy. Pale."

After the meeting, Haley slowly walked alone back to the office. She had fifty minutes before Val's session. *A big, soft white guy who was pale.*

Had Eli Loomis been in the Alexion building? Maybe he came to pick her up after work, and she couldn't remember. Brenda at the front desk might know. She hurried inside to find out.

Chapter Fourteen

Brenda took a look at Eli's photo and said, "I've never seen him in my life. If he came in, I wasn't working that day."

Haley spent the next half hour going through her client list again, this time looking for someone big who also had a beef with her. She narrowed her list down to three people.

She texted Daylon: It's either Eli Loomis, Jovan Jansen or Scott Blankenship.

He replied: I have news. See you later.

She smiled as she put her phone away. A man of few words.

Val arrived for her session a little out of breath. She had on a hot pink dress with a flared skirt that landed above the knee. "I was afraid I would be late," she said. "I had a conference call that ran over."

Haley waited for her to settle in, then gave her usual opener. "How have things been going?"

"Great!" Val gave her a gleaming smile. "I've met someone."

"Whoa," Haley said, smiling back. "Who is it?"

"He's a diamond-level distributor with my company. I met him at the meeting in Scranton. We went out for dinner, then lunch the next day, and…he's been calling me ever since." She touched her neck. "Last weekend, he drove over."

"And…?"

"And he stayed with me all weekend." Val sighed with a faraway look in her eyes. "It was magic, Haley. We have so much in common."

"I'm glad for you," Haley said. "It's nice to hear good news in this office. So, tell me about him..."

Val spent the next twenty minutes giving her a detailed rundown—early 50s, divorced with two teenage boys who lived with their mother and, of course, the usual words *funny, handsome* and *romantic* that always showed up at the beginning and disappeared in the end.

As their time ran out, Haley asked, "How is Jovan? Do you hear from him?"

Val made a face. "All I know is he's working for the phone company, and he lives somewhere east of Canaburgh. I haven't heard from him in months. I hope I never do for the rest of my life!"

After Val left, Haley stayed in the wingback chair. Was that how she saw Daylon—funny, handsome and romantic? He did make her laugh. Handsome...yeah, but romantic...not the flowers and late-night phone calls version of romantic. He didn't dress to impress or show up in a flashy car to take her out for fine dining. Daylon was different, and she felt different around him. He was comfortable. That was his word, *comfortable*. She moved her head side to side, savoring the word. *Comfortable*. She liked it.

Picking up the landline phone in her office, she dialed a colleague who had a practice twenty minutes away. It was time for her to see someone and sort out all the stuff swirling around in her brain. Actually, it was probably past time.

Her second call was to the security company.

When she arrived home shortly before six, the garage door stood open. She eased the car inside. When she got out, Daylon strolled up and handed her a black box with a clip attached to it.

"For your visor," he said.

"Oh, a garage clicker thing." She opened the car door and slid it into place.

"Your place or mine?" he said. "A lot happened today. We need to catch up."

"I should have made a list. I have so much to tell you." She pinned him with a look. "Starting with calling you a blabbermouth."

He glanced away and back. "Sonia."

"Sonia indeed." Haley reached up for a kiss. "It was bound to happen." She told him about the private confab in Sonia's office. "She said you looked so happy, she forced you to tell her why."

He pulled her into a hug and kissed her for real. Touching his forehead to hers, he whispered, "Sonia is a very smart lady."

Haley laughed and let her cheek snuggle against his flannel shirt for a few seconds. Turning him loose, she said, "Do you have anything in the fridge? Mine is pretty empty tonight."

"Let's call out for Chinese."

"In that case, your place." She headed toward the stairs. "I'll be down in a few minutes."

"Bring your toothbrush," he called after her. He pulled down the garage door.

When she returned, he had the dining room table set up with notes and his laptop. Two glasses of iced tea stood ready. She dropped her purse next to the lounge chair. "Wow. This looks serious."

"I told you," he said. "Today, I had an idea of how we can smoke him out. We'll seed the pond and watch him take the bait."

She waited for him to go on.

"You have a direct line to him on your phone," he said. "All

166

you have to do is send him a reply text that will tick him off. We'll catch him when he shows up."

She huffed out a short breath. "Under normal circumstances, I would *never* try something like that."

"Seven people who live on this street have volunteered to set up a perimeter and box him in when he shows up. Five are ex-military."

"I don't want anyone to get hurt, Daylon. I couldn't live with myself if someone got hurt because of me."

His chin came up and so did his volume. "None of this is happening because of you. Everything that's happening is because he's a *sorry coward* who preys on women."

The doorbell rang.

"That's dinner," he said and went to the door.

While they ate, Haley said, "Cheri did a reading on the street video today."

"Did she get his name and address?" He opened his mouth wide to fit in a bundle of noodles wrapped around his fork.

She tapped his chest with the back of her fingers. "No, Smartypants." She told him what Cheri had seen. "That's how I came up with the three names in my text, although I can't remember whether Eli Loomis ever came to the office. I don't think so. Ditto for Scott Blankenship. I left those two on the list in case I'm forgetting something."

"That leaves...?"

"Jovan Jansen, a former client who came to me along with his wife...for marriage counselling. Long story short, they ended up getting a divorce anyway. He sued me shortly after New Year's, but the judge threw out his case for lack of evidence. From what Val said, he was so angry he almost stroked out."

"Why stalk you? Why not go after his wife?"

167

"She has two restraining orders out on him. If he goes near her, he goes to jail. As long as he stays anonymous, he can take all his frustration out on me and get away with it."

"Not for long." He pushed the legal pad toward her. "Write out everything you know about him, so I can check him out. Meanwhile, think of something you can say to him that will bring him here."

"Isn't that entrapment?"

"Not the way we're going to do it."

She wrote down what she could remember about Jovan. She handed him the page. "I'll text you more when I can read my files tomorrow. I have an installation appointment with a security company on Friday morning between seven and nine a.m. I told them about the situation, so they bumped me up."

"Who is it?"

"The company Conley Carpenter works for. They have the security service at Alexion and the bookstore. Both Cheri and Sonia vouched for them, so I called them."

He gathered empty food cartons and stacked them together. "You have been busy. Anything else?"

"Oh yeah, Linda is looking for a private investigator to check up on her soon-to-be-ex-husband. Sonia gave her your number."

He leaned over to put his arms around her. "You are a woman of many talents."

She turned her head to nuzzle his ear and whisper, "You haven't seen anything yet."

The stalker was the last thing on their minds for the rest of the night.

The next morning, Haley stopped by Frankie's office and found her sitting at her desk.

Haley said, "I'm glad I caught you. You have something for

me?"

Frankie flipped her braids with a graceful movement of her slim fingers. "Yes, I do." She reached under her desk and pulled out some folded fabric. She handed it to Haley. "I made this for you."

Haley set down her purse to take a look. It was a tunic made of scrunchy royal blue fabric with pale blue embroidered flowers in a spray starting at the lower right and going across to the left shoulder. Feeling the softness in her hands, Haley fell instantly in love. "Frankie, this is beautiful! You made this for me? It must have taken hours and hours."

"I must keep my hands busy, so I might as well do this."

"I want to put it on. I'll be right back." She hurried to her empty office and closed the door. As soon as the cotton garment fell around her, Haley sighed with pleasure and gently stretched her back, feeling the fabric move with her. She eyed the silk blouse and jacket she had just taken off. No way was she putting them back on when this felt so good.

She grabbed her key fob and took her clothes to the car. When she came back, Frankie and Cheri were in the hall. "Look!" she said, holding her arms wide and turning. "It's so comfortable!"

Cheri said, "That color is perfect on you. It makes your eyes shine." She smiled at Frankie. "You, my dear, are missing your true calling. I'm telling you."

Haley hurried for a hug. "Thank you so much, Frankie. I want to talk to you about making me more of these."

A client came through the back door. They headed their separate ways, and their day began.

Haley's first appointment was Joey Everly, but he didn't appear. After fifteen minutes, Haley called his cellphone. He didn't pick up.

She texted him: Did you forget your 10:00 appt? I can see you at 5:00 today, if that's better for you. Give me a call.

No reply.

One missed appointment wasn't an emergency. It happened.

The next morning, a tap on her door brought Haley out of her bedroom. She was dressed for work but still had bare feet. Daylon had already gone downstairs.

She looked through the miniblinds on her living room window and saw Conley Carpenter and another guy checking out the cameras on her verandah. They wore blue uniforms with name badges and tool belts.

As wide and tall as a football player, Conley had frizzy red hair like his grandmother, Cheri. He kept it short except for a snarl of curls on top. His co-worker looked like the actor Kevin James, only taller.

Haley pushed her feet into slippers and hurried to open the door. "Conley! How are you?"

He grinned, and his freckled cheeks dimpled. "I'm good, Haley." He grew serious. "Frankie tells me you've been having some trouble." He nodded toward the guy with him. "This is Nick. He's going to work outside to hook into the system." He lifted the clipboard he held by his side. "Let's take care of the paperwork."

She pulled the door wider to let him step past her before she closed the door. She sank into the lounge chair and waved toward the sofa. "Please, sit down."

He took her information and had her choose her code and safe word. As they were wrapping up, Haley said, "You belong to the Steampunk Club. Is that right?"

Nodding, Conley hooked his pen through a slot on the

170

clipboard and waited for her to go on.

"Do you know Joey Everly?"

"Sure. He comes over sometimes to use my forge. How do you know Joey?"

"A friend of mine died a few weeks ago—Flo Yeager. Did you hear about that?"

When he nodded, she went on, "Cheri, Frankie and I went over there one day, and we met Joey. He lives next door. He's a friend of the family."

"Friend of the family?" Conley said, wrinkling his forehead. "He's more than a friend of the family."

Haley said, "What do you mean?"

"He was obsessed with Flo. He couldn't stop talking about her and not in a good way. He keeps going on about how Flo is a domineering mother, how she suffocates Fleeta and a lot of other things I'd rather not go into." He handed Haley the homeowner's information booklet and stood up. "Joey's a nice guy, but he's a little weird. He hides it well most of the time, but he's got issues."

Daylon tapped on the door, and Haley let him in. She said, "Cheri's grandson, Conley, is here for the install. Do you know each other?"

Daylon shook Conley's hand. "Daylon Jasper. I've seen you around, but I don't think we've ever met."

Haley interrupted Daylon by placing her hand on his back. "I don't want to be rude, but I have to get to work. I'll let you guys take care of the details."

She told Conley, "He knows more about everything than I do, and you can tell him anything you'd tell me." She smiled at Conley. "Great to see you again."

"I think we're done here anyway," he replied. "I'll check on the outside hookup."

171

As Conley left, Haley went to a drawer and found her spare key. She handed it to Daylon. "You'll need a key if they need to get inside again."

"I already have a spare," he said, "in case a pipe breaks when you're not home or something.

"But you always knock."

"In case you're not decent," he said, then grinned at the irony of that statement.

She gave him an arch look and gently pushed him toward the door. "A tiny bit on the slow side, don't you think?"

Still chuckling, he closed the door behind him.

Switching her slippers for comfortable shoes, Haley found Detective Banks's number on her business phone and called him.

Chapter Fifteen

When Detective Banks picked up, she said, "I just came across some information you should know about. A friend of Joey Everly told me that Joey resented Flo Yeager. He thought she was a domineering mother and treated Fleeta badly."

The detective replied, "What is your relationship to Joseph Everly?"

"I can't tell you that."

"Oh, so he's a client. Thanks for calling, Ms. Meyers. We will definitely check that out today."

Haley put finishing touches on her hair and makeup and headed downstairs. Daylon and Conley had the garage door open when she reached her car. Daylon came over to kiss her good-bye. He stood watching as she carefully backed out of the driveway.

Joey resented Flo? How did she miss that? She counted on her intuition to let her in on things like that. How could she have missed something so big and so important? And why did Fleeta leave that out of her statements?

Shortly before eleven, Haley got a call from Barb. Her voice sounded ragged. "The cops are all over Joey's house, at least eight police cars and more coming."

"Have you seen Joey?"

"No. I just came home to pick something up and saw the commotion. I have to get right back to the cafe."

"Thanks, Babe. Let's catch up later, okay?"

"Sure, whenever you can get away from your new honey," Barb said with a soft chuckle. She went on, more serious. "I've always liked Daylon. He's a good guy. He used to come in twice a week, but now I don't see him much. You are bad for business."

Haley smiled. "The four of us should get together on the weekend. I might even cook."

"Promises, promises," Barb said. "I'm putting in an order for your beef stew right now. Make plenty, so we can bring home lots of leftovers."

Their words were lighthearted, but they were actually blowing off steam in an intense situation. When you've been best friends for more than thirty years, most of the conversation is in subtext. Other relationships might come and go, but Barb and Haley were bonded for life.

Finishing the call, Haley set her phone on her desk. Everything in her wanted to rush over to see what was happening at Joey's house.

He didn't mean it. Was she remembering Cheri's words or was Flo sending her a message? She couldn't figure it out, so she let it go for now. She had one more client before she could go over to Joey's on her lunch hour.

When Haley arrived at Joey's house, four patrol cars remained on the street. Everyone else had left. Thinking she would find out where they were holding Joey, she knocked and a uniformed officer opened the door.

"I'm here to see Detective Banks," Haley said.

The officer went back inside and a moment later, Detective Banks stepped outside. He closed the door behind him.

"Can I see Joey today?" she asked. "Where are you holding him?"

He didn't answer for a moment, then he said, "Joey's body

174

was found in the park behind the house. He jumped or was pushed from the bridge and broke his neck."

The world reeled for a second. She took a tiny step back, one hand pressed across her mouth, the other on her heart. She couldn't breathe.

Detective Banks reached out to steady her.

Haley tried to swallow. Her throat felt like it was closing. She gasped, "I have to get some water."

"I can't let you inside until we process the house," he said. "I'm sorry."

She turned away from him. "I have water in my car," she croaked. She felt lightheaded.

"Do you want someone to drive you home?"

She held up her hand, palm outward, and rasped out, "Thank you, Detective. Thank you for letting me know."

She managed to reach the driver's seat before her knees gave out. Sipping from her water bottle, she sat a long time with her head against the headrest. Somehow, she hadn't asked the right questions. How could she have missed so much?

Finally, she headed home.

Death was a frequent theme in her work with clients, as was every part of the human experience. But two clients dead under suspicious circumstances—this was surreal. She had her own appointment for a counselling session on Monday, and she wished it were today.

Daylon's truck was gone when she reached the house.

She closed her blinds and curled up on the sofa, staring at nothing, hardly breathing. She dreamed of someone knocking and slowly surfaced enough to realize Daylon was at her door.

"Haley!" he called. "Are you in there?"

Blinking, she opened the door to see his hand level with her forehead, about to knock again. He pulled her into his arms. "I was worried. I've been knocking, and you didn't answer."

Her voice quivered. "Joey's body was found this afternoon. He's dead." A gasp gushed out of her like a sob from her soul.

Daylon held her until the storm subsided. Finally, he murmured. "Let's go in, okay?"

Nodding, she stepped inside and returned to the sofa. He flipped on the kitchen light. "Would you like some tea?" he asked.

"I would like some company," she said, patting the seat next to her.

He sat close and wrapped his arms around her. She snuggled her head into the curve of his neck. "So much loss," she said. "Flo lost her life. Fleeta lost her mother. Joey lost...everything. It's hard to understand why things like this happen."

His voice sounded soft against her hair. "Maybe we're not meant to understand it," he said.

She melted against him, suddenly incredibly sleepy. "We're not so different in what we believe after all, are we?"

He relaxed against the back of the sofa, and she relaxed into him. When she woke up, it was dark. Daylon still had his arms around her, his head leaning straight back and his mouth wide open, sound asleep. Her throat was so dry, she felt like she would choke if she didn't get a drink.

When she moved, Daylon stirred and let her go. He rubbed his face with both hands. "I knocked out. What time is it?"

"Nine-thirty," she said, heading for the fridge. "Do you want some water or some tea?"

"Water," he said. When she came back with their glasses, he asked, "What happened? Are you ready to talk about it?"

"Yeah. I'm okay now." She told him about Conley's

comment that morning about Joey's distaste for Flo, followed by her call to Detective Banks. "Barb called me at work to say the cops were swarming Joey's house. I thought they were arresting him, so I went over there."

"And they told you he was gone."

She nodded. "When Banks told me, I pretty much lost it." She waved her hand to erase that. "I mean, I knew I had to come home." She drank the rest of her water and set the glass on the coffee table.

He said, "Do you want me to go now? You want to be alone?"

She focused on him with new appreciation. "As much as I love having you around, I'm going to say yes. I feel like I need to lie down, put on a meditation audio and get some sound sleep. Do you mind?"

"Not at all." He kissed her cheek. "If you need anything, just text me, okay?"

He went to get up, but she held him back. "I didn't break down until you got here," she said. "Thank you for being there for me...for letting me get it all out without trying to talk me down." Her eyes filled. "I hear words all day long and sometimes I just need space with no words."

His expression softened. He gathered her to him for a long squeeze. "I could say the same to you, Haley Meyers. Thank you for being there for me." A few seconds later, he let her go and moved to stand. "I'd better get out of here now, or I won't be going anywhere."

She pulled him back, more insistent this time. "I think I just changed my mind."

In one move he laid her back full length on the sofa. For the next hour, she was smothered and covered and taken and cherished. This went far beyond the blending of bodies to the melding of souls. She had never felt so loved and so seen in her entire life.

They stayed quiet for a long time, full-body, skin-to-skin, in a warm trance too deep for conversation. Wedged against the back of the sofa, he had his arm up with his head resting on the crook of his elbow, her head nestled into his neck.

A violent crash. Glass sprayed over them. A wooden chair turned over.

He shielded Haley. "Don't open your eyes! You have glass on your cheek."

She pressed against him, her heart pounding. "What happened?"

"Something came through the window. Stay still, okay? I have to check outside. Keep your eyes closed. I'll be right back." He was off the sofa in a single move. "Ow!"

"Daylon?" she cried out.

"Glass in my foot. It's not bad. Stay there. Don't open your eyes. I'll be right back."

In a moment he returned. "I have your slippers. Let's get you to the shower to wash the glass off your face."

The water sprayed, and she carefully moved into the shower, feeling the walls to orient herself. Gently, she explored her face with her fingertips. Her left cheek was on fire. So was her left shoulder and hip. She touched her hair and immediately nicked her finger. She didn't know how to move without hurting herself, so she stayed perfectly still.

Daylon slid into the shower behind her. "Let me help you," he said, passing his fingers lightly over her cheeks and forehead, letting the water wash the slivers away. "Stand still," he said. "Glass is washing down to the floor."

"Is he gone?"

"Yes. The police are on their way."

"I'm so mad at them! Why don't they do something?"

"You can open your eyes now."

She peeked at him through the shower spray. "You're bleeding!" He had cuts on his shoulders. He turned, and his back had more than a dozen wounds. "You have two pieces of glass sticking out of your back!"

He braced himself, hands against the back wall of the shower. "Pull them out, Haley. Just don't cut yourself."

She managed to get a grip with her fingernails and carefully removed them. She pressed the pieces into the soap dish, so they wouldn't wash to the floor to be stepped on. Red rivulets ran down his back. "You need bandages."

"Do they need stitches?"

"I don't think so. They weren't very deep, thank God."

"Bandages can wait." He pulled the handheld shower head down to spray the shower floor clear of glass. "Right now, I need to go downstairs for a clean t-shirt and some pants, so I can talk to the cops. My clothes are covered in glass. I can't put them back on. Dammit. Those were my favorite jeans." He hooked the showerhead to the wall.

Haley said, "Take my terrycloth robe. It's on the back of the door."

"I'll get blood on it."

"Take it!"

He did just that and was gone. Haley gave her hair and her body a final rinse and turned off the water. As she wiped the steam from the mirror, the seriousness of the situation hit her full force. The left side of her face had tiny cuts as well as her left shoulder, arm and hip, too many to count. She grabbed her brush and bent over the sink, brushing her hair. Falling bits of glass covered the sink. She used a damp tissue to wipe them out.

What if they had been sitting on the sofa and the brick had hit one of them in the head? What if all this glass had gone into their necks? What would that psycho do next?

Her hands started shaking. She shuddered and hurried to her closet to find warm clothes. She was pulling on her shoes when Daylon came back wearing a washed-out t-shirt and paint-speckled jeans.

"The cops are here," he said. "They're in the living room looking at the damage. I called Martin to let him know they'll need to replace the window."

Haley stood up and put her arms around him, holding on to steady herself. In a moment, he said, "Ready?"

They went out, and Haley drew up in the doorway of the living room, overwhelmed at the destruction. The miniblinds hung in tatters. It moved in the breeze showing the window frame, empty except for a few shards that clung to the edges. Jagged bits of glass covered her sofa and spread all the way across the laminate flooring in the kitchen. A brick lay on top of an overturned dining chair with two of the slats cracked. It matched the extra-wide red brick that had shattered her car window.

Sgt. Kirk was bent over, taking pictures. With him was a female officer who looked like the tough-girl version of Jennifer Lopez. She had on white latex gloves. When she came over to Haley, she said, "I'm Corporal Alvarez. Are you the homeowner?" She had a clipboard and a pen ready to take notes.

"Renter," Haley said. "I live here, yes."

"Please tell me what happened."

"We were on the sofa, and the brick came through the

180

window. It's a miracle someone wasn't hurt!"

"Did you see anyone?"

"No. It happened so fast. Daylon ran outside, and I stayed here. I had glass on my face, so I went to wash it off before it got into my eyes."

"We're calling this reckless endangerment," she said. "You're right. Someone could have been killed." She looked at Daylon. "Text us that video footage ASAP."

The officers stayed a few minutes longer, then went outside.

Still in the doorway, Haley stared at the mess. "It's going to take forever to get this cleaned up." The back of Daylon's shirt had two shiny red circles about the size of silver dollars. "You've got to let me take care of those cuts," she said.

"Let's wait on that. I want to cover that window. It's not safe to leave it open with a nutcase out there. I have a piece of plywood in the garage."

"What if he's out there waiting for you?"

"The police are still here. They're looking around the lawn. That's why I need to do it now." He disappeared out the door.

She took a broom from the hall closet and swept up dustpan after dustpan of broken glass, not only the window but their drinking glasses also lay in shards. Kneeling on a piece of cardboard to keep from getting more cuts, she went over every inch of laminate flooring with damp paper towels to get up the slivers. She glanced at the gray area-rug in front of the sofa. That would have to go.

Oh no! The sofa was cloth, too. What a nightmare.

Half an hour later, Daylon stood in her bathroom while Haley butterflied and bandaged the worst of his cuts. By some miracle, he didn't need stitches.

He said, "I feel like he's always one step ahead of us. While

I'm working out a way to catch him, he strikes again."

She tore off a strip of white tape. "You're learning," she drawled.

He grunted.

She dropped the tape roll into a drawer and closed it with a thump. "I'm going to be combing glass out of my hair for the next month."

He turned to hug her. "When I think about what might have happened…" He lost his breath for a second. "Until we catch this guy, you'll sleep at my place, okay?"

She frowned. "I really like my own bed."

"It won't be for long. I have a plan."

Chapter Sixteen

"What's your plan?" Haley asked.

"Shock and awe, baby. Shock and awe." Daylon reached for his shirt. "It's almost midnight. Grab what you need for the night. While you do that, I'm going to send the security video to the cops. We have to get some sleep."

Before they turned in, Daylon showed her twenty seconds of video from the upstairs camera. Someone had set off the motion lights and still crept up the stairs. Even with the lights on, all they could see of him was a black form. He stayed hunched down with his head low and never looked up. The minute he threw the brick, he scuttled down the steps and out of camera range.

When they got into bed, Daylon moved close to her back. She relaxed against him, glad to feel him next to her, keeping her warm whenever she started shivering with nerves. She dozed fitfully and woke up to see light coming from the open bathroom door.

No sense staying in bed any longer. More sleep was only wishful thinking.

Daylon had lined his sink with paper towels and was bent over it combing glass out of his hair. Wearing a long sleep shirt, she leaned against the doorjamb.

When he noticed her, he said, "We're going to have to get rid of those sheets." He winced as he drew the comb through. "I didn't think about my hair still having glass in it until I looked at my pillow this morning."

She held out her hand to take the comb from him. "I can see better than you can."

He waited with his eyes closed while she gently guided the comb. "I could get a buzz cut," he said.

"What a shame. You've got great hair. I'm sure Martin Summers would kill for this hair." She worked in silence for a few minutes, then said, "I never realized how much trouble someone could cause—stealing time and money and emotional energy from someone—and for what? Revenge? Settling some sort of grievance? How much satisfaction can someone get from hurting people? It's crazy."

His voice grew intense. "I don't have any patience for someone who won't just come out with what's bothering them and get it settled. This hit-and-run thing shows they are too weak to manage their problems like an adult."

"Maybe they have mental health issues."

"In that case, they are a danger to others, and they need to be put somewhere safe."

"I'm with you," she said, moving to the other side. "Believe me, I've had all the fun I can stand."

"I've set up a meeting this morning with the volunteers in the neighborhood. We're going to get together in the park behind the school."

"How can I help?" she asked.

"I won't know until after the meeting. I'll tell you tonight." He reached up and took the comb from her. "That's enough for now."

"You better rinse off in the shower," she said. "You have glass on your skin. When you get out, I'll change the bandages."

While he stood in the tub with the handheld shower head carefully rinsing his face and neck, she leaned over the sink to comb through her own hair. "When are you planning to pull all this off and catch the guy?" she yelled above the sound of running water.

"Maybe tonight, or tomorrow night at the latest."

"I have a break from eleven to one today, so call me and fill me in, okay?"

Carefully folding the paper towels to keep the glass inside, she pushed it into the trash can beside the sink. Daylon shoved aside the curtain and reached for the blue towel hanging nearby.

A few minutes later, she finished the last bandage and went to the bedroom to pull on her lounge pants. "I need to go upstairs and get dressed for work. I don't feel like breakfast today. I'll get coffee at the office."

Holding his shirt scrunched up, ready to stretch it over his head, he leaned toward her for a kiss. "I'll call you later."

The rest of the day, Haley went through the usual motions, but her mind was on Daylon and his plan. He was in his element, and she was way out of hers. The best thing for her to do at this point was to stay distracted enough to keep her mind from going to dark places and countless what-if's.

Frankie stopped Haley in the hall. "What happened to your face?" she demanded.

Cheri heard her and joined them. Her mouth went open when she saw Haley.

"The stalker threw a brick through my living room window last night. Thank God, no one was seriously hurt."

Cheri said, "You called the police?"

"The security system called them, and they are the most *worthless*...!" She glanced toward the waiting room where a woman in an orange yoga outfit was talking to Brenda. Lowering her voice, she went on, "The police weren't much help, let's just

185

put it that way."

"You should come and stay with me," Cheri said. "You're not safe there."

"I'm staying at Daylon's place tonight," Haley said. "Hopefully, this will be over soon." She touched both ladies. "Please send angelic protection. I'd really appreciate that!" Her next client arrived, and she went to greet them.

Daylon called her a few minutes past eleven. "We're on for tonight," he said. "Those guys are great. We need to have them over for a cookout sometime. You would like them. We're going to start the stakeout tonight, but who knows when he'll show up." He paused. "I have two things for you to do, if you want to."

"Of course. What are they?"

"Send the stalker a reply text that will smoke him out. Make him want to come back. You have to be careful what you say because the cops are going to look at that text. Make it something indirect and not too inflammatory."

"Hmmm… I'll think about that. What else?"

"As part of the Shock and Awe plan, we thought it might be good to have a big noise go off when the lights turn on. Everyone was totally against a motion-detected alarm. I figured that. I'm thinking maybe a couple of Bluetooth speakers operated by a phone. Any electronics store should have that. I have to be here at the house when the new window is delivered, so I'm not sure I'll have time to go to the store. Can you take care of that?"

"Sure. So, text him and pick up speakers. I'll pick up something for dinner, too."

"You think of everything," he said, a smile in his voice. "Be careful, Haley. See you tonight."

She sat back in her desk chair, thinking of what she could text. Grabbing her purse, she headed to her car. She had almost two hours until her next appointment. She could pick up the speakers while she thought about the text message.

Heading west through town, she caught sight of a pool supply sign at the end of the street. She pulled into their gravel parking lot. Suddenly, she had a flash of inspiration. She quickly picked up her cell phone and pulled up the text window. She spoke five words into her phone and hit Send.

The inside of the pool store was overcrowded with boxes sitting around the walls. The shelves had a thin layer of dust. A big guy sat on a stool behind a high counter. He had a pile of empty candy wrappers and a half-eaten hamburger lying near his elbow. Without speaking, he raised his bushy eyebrows at her while sipping soda from a large plastic cup.

"I'm looking for speakers that put out a lot of sound and can tolerate any weather. When I saw your sign, I remembered a friend of mine used to have a speaker floating in the pool. Do you have anything like that?"

He nodded and wiped ketchup off his mouth with a crumpled napkin. "Sure. Aisle Four, about halfway down."

She looked over the selection and stopped at a blue ball. It was about six inches in diameter and looked like a plastic toy, solid on the bottom and dimpled on top. She picked up three boxes and returned to the desk. "Can you demonstrate one of these for me? I want to hear the sound."

He reached behind him and brought up a matching blue ball. It had a hook hidden on one side that could be used to anchor it. Pulling up a screen on his phone, he touched a button and "Black Magic Woman" rattled the windows. After a few bars of music, he turned it off.

She nodded. "I'll take these," she said, moving the boxes on the counter closer to him.

"Anything else?"

"Yes, you can help me connect them to my phone." She looked around. "Do you have zip ties?"

Twenty minutes later, she left with a large brown bag. In the car, she spoke into her phone to text Daylon: Mission accomplished. See you tonight.

Daylon: The window just arrived. See you later.

Before she put her phone away, a text came through from Detective Banks: Please come to the station tomorrow afternoon at four pm to make a statement about Joey Everly.

She texted back: I have an hour free. Can I come over now?

He replied with a thumbs up.

Haley stopped at her office to grab Joey's file and headed to the police station. The receptionist took her back right away. While she was waiting for the detectives, she opened the file. Folded pages from a yellow legal pad lay on top. Opening them, she began to read.

She was still reading when Detective Banks came in. "You need to see this," she said, handing him the pages.

"Put them on the table for me," he said. "What is this?"

She told him about Joey journaling while in her office. "He forgot these, so I put them in his file. I forgot about them until now."

Using his pen to separate the pages, he scanned the block writing, then went to the door and called to an officer. They spoke privately for a moment, then Banks came back. He pulled gloves from his pocket and slid the pages into an evidence bag.

The words on one page burned into Haley's mind.

Fleeta and I are going to run away together as soon as the coast is clear. Her mother, a.k.a. Mommy Dearest, wouldn't let us be together, so we had to get rid of her. Now her dad is pulling the same crap. Fleeta says we might have to get rid of him, too. I don't know if I can do it again. The first time was awful, but Fleeta said we have to do what we have to do.

What's wrong with him? The only place we can be together is the park. We have to sneak out at night and meet on the bridge. It's crazy. He is crazy.

I can't sleep and my medication isn't doing much good either. I don't know how much longer I can hold out. If I have to go into the hospital again, I might end up confessing. Fleeta would be so mad at me if I did that.

Haley was on her way back to her car when a police cruiser parked near the curb. An officer got out and led Fleeta inside. She was cuffed and swearing loudly, unrecognizable as the grieving girl Haley thought she knew.

Haley stopped and stared until they went through the double glass doors. She could understand misjudging Joey. She hardly knew him. But Fleeta? She had worked closely with this girl for more than a year. Did her years of training and experience mean anything at all?

Trying to unlock her car, she fumbled the key fob, dropped it and finally got it open. She desperately needed a vacation.

When Haley came through the backdoor of Alexion, Linda was in the waiting room. She strode down the hall aimed right at Haley. "I've got an appointment with your boyfriend," she blurted out. "On Monday."

"My boyfriend? I never liked that word. He's not a boy, and he's not my friend."

Linda frowned and went on as though Haley hadn't spoken. "I had no idea how tough a divorce was going to be. If it were just me, it would be different. But my kids..." She grimaced. "They're going through a lot right now."

"It's not easy," Haley murmured, sympathy in her voice. "But you'll get through it and be glad in the end. From one who knows."

Linda glanced at her phone. "I've got to go. I just came by to say thanks, Haley." She gave her a hug. "It's going to be okay," she said, as though speaking for Haley, then she hurried toward the State Street side of the building and dashed out.

Somehow Haley got through her afternoon appointments. Before her last client arrived, she pulled up the app to Barb's café and ordered two meals—one mac-and-cheese and one barbequed chicken with two salads on the side. When she was done for the day, she walked across the street to pick up the order. Barb wasn't in the restaurant, so a few minutes later she headed down the alley to her car with a big bag in her hands.

When she reached home, she loaded both arms with packages. Before she could tap the door with her foot, Daylon rushed out and took the food from her.

"Thanks! I was about to drop everything…" She stared at him in disbelief.

He wore the same blue flannel shirt that lay on the floor covered in glass a few hours ago.

"You put that shirt back on?" she demanded.

He chuckled. "I have three of these," he said. "Once I found out how comfortable they were, I went back and bought two more. Now, I'm glad I did. I wish I could say the same about my favorite jeans."

"And you were going to tell me all this, when? Ever since we met, I thought you were washing every night and putting the same shirt back on." She shook her head.

"If it's not broke, don't fix it," he said. "I happen to like this shirt."

"So, do I," she said, reaching out to rub his arm.

"Keep doing that, and I'll follow you anywhere."

She laughed. "Let's eat while the food is hot," she said. "I asked the guy at the store to hook the speakers to my phone. They're all ready to go."

He opened a container. "Mac-and-cheese! I'm starving. I haven't eaten all day."

"Me neither. I spent my lunch hour shopping."

They dished up the food and sat close together on his sofa to eat. A few minutes later, Daylon said, "What did you end up texting him?"

She found the text and handed him the phone.

He read it, frowned, looked at her and read it aloud. "Yo mama is a toaster?"

"What?" She took the phone back. "I meant to say, 'Yo mama is a toker.' Stupid spellcheck. I got nervous thinking about him reading what I sent and what might happen. I didn't read it before I sent it."

He burst out laughing, then repeated under his breath, "Yo mama is a toaster." He picked up the phone and read it again. "Well, anything that starts with *Yo mama* will make a guy mad, I guess." His chest jiggled. He reached over to kiss her temple.

"So, what happens now?" she asked.

"Let's get those speakers set up and then we take a nap. It could be a long night."

She pulled out boxes. "I got three of them. They have a range of fifty feet."

"We'll put one on the garage, one on the verandah and one on the tree by the street. That should blast him out pretty good."

At a few minutes before eleven, the team of volunteers formed a circle around the outer edges of the property—around the garage, the back of the house and under the shadow of the fir tree near the street. Daylon was out of sight in the back of his truck.

Haley observed from inside Daylon's front window. She had her phone cued up and ready. She had wanted to be outside with everyone else, but Daylon was firm, "You are his target. He's going to zero in on you, and this time he might have more with him than a brick."

He did have a point. So, she watched from the window. As soon as the lights went on in the driveway, she would blast the noise and give them a few extra seconds to tackle the guy.

She turned out the lights inside Daylon's apartment with a light in the hall closet giving her enough of a glow to get around without falling over furniture. She stood by the window for a few minutes. Her mouth felt dry. She left the window to fill a glass with water and brought the glass back with her. She dragged a chair from the table and sat where she could still see.

Suddenly, Dad stood beside her.

She put her hand out and felt a chill as it passed through his leg. "Hmmm, cold. It feels like putting my hand inside the refrigerator."

"At least you're not jumping out of your skin whenever I show up," he said.

"You're growing on me," she said, beaming at him. Glancing out the window, she went on, "This stalker has changed my entire perspective. Don't take anything for granted. Don't be too trusting. Don't overshare your information. I don't see that as an improvement, Dad. I'd rather go on naive and innocent."

"That's not how the world is, though. Is it?"

She shook her head. "Sadly, no."

"Don't forget one very important good thing that came of all this…"

She nodded. "Daylon."

"Isn't that the way of it? Some good comes with the bad and some bad comes with the good?"

Suddenly, the driveway lit up.

She hit the button, and Steven Tyler screeched, "Because nobody believes me. The man was such a sleeze, He ain't never gonna be the sa-a-ame!'…Janie's got a gun…"

Scuffling and shouts. A man roared with rage. Haley peered out the window. Daylon and another man had someone on the ground.

She reached the driveway in time to see Daylon pull a black ski mask off of a guy kissing the pavement. He had puffy cheeks and a wild look in his eyes. A fat red brick lay on the ground a short distance away.

Haley gasped. She recognized him.

"Nick Ortolano," Daylon said, scorn in every word. "Who else?"

Haley said, "He was here with Conley to put in the security system."

"He's the last guy who lived in your apartment."

Red faced and heaving, Nick glared at Haley. "That's MY apartment. You stupid cow! Can't you take a hint? You think you can just move into someone's house like it doesn't matter?" He kept shouting while Daylon put a black zip tie around his wrists.

Blue and red lights flashed at the end of the street, and their volunteers faded into the darkness.

"You can turn off the music," Daylon said, keeping his boot on the man's lower back, so he couldn't get up.

She touched a button, and Steven Tyler stopped in mid-scream. The only sound left was sirens coming to their rescue.

193

Sgt. Kirk got out of the patrol car and strolled up. When he saw the man in black lying at their feet, he smirked. "Well, well, well. You finally got him."

Daylon said, "He used to live in Haley's apartment. He was trying to scare her away."

"She has no right!" Nick shouted, struggling with his bonds. "That's my apartment! I lived there for nine years! They can't throw me out!"

Sgt. Kirk shook his head and made eye contact with Haley. "He needs help, and he's going to get it." Leaning down, he grabbed Nick's arms and brought him to his feet in one motion. He placed cuffs on his wrists and cut loose the zip tie.

"You haven't seen the last of me!" Nick screamed. "I'll do more than break a few windows next time!"

"Go ahead. Get it off your chest. Just keep on talking," Sgt. Kirk said as he led him to the patrol car and put him inside.

He came back to slide the brick into a brown paper bag. "I don't think we'll have any problem making charges stick. I'll text you if we need anything more from you, but I doubt it." He put the evidence bag in the trunk and got into the car.

After the patrol car disappeared, Haley and Daylon stayed in the driveway, gazing down the empty street. The streetlights made yellow circles on the sidewalks. The night breeze lifted her hair and cooled her neck.

She glanced up at him. "I can't believe how far off base I was. His name wasn't even on the list."

"See what I mean?" Daylon said, coming behind her to wrap his arms around her waist. "When you think you have an answer, other possibilities disappear."

She leaned back, basking his nearness. "No wonder he knew how to get around the cameras. He had professional training."

"And that's how he got your private phone number, and a lot of other things…" He leaned down to put his cheek next to hers. "It's a good thing you didn't sign up for the service sooner. He would have been able to track your every move."

"As bad as it was, it could have been so much worse. I could have been alone going through it." She rested her head back against his chest, listening to the crickets and feeling the quietness of the night.

Suddenly, she gasped and pulled away to look at him. "I'm going to have to get rid of that sofa and the area rug. They're full of glass." She groaned. "I love that sofa!"

"You can always move in with me," he said, half teasing and half not. "Think of how much trouble it would save you. You wouldn't have to replace the furniture... You could save yourself all that rent…"

"Uhmmm…you're kind of pushing things, don't you think?"

"Too soon?" he asked, a grin in his voice.

Dad's voice came from the stairs. "Way too soon!"

Haley chuckled. "Smartypants."

Epilogue

Six weeks later, Haley was on her way to work when her phone rang. She hit the phone button on her steering wheel, and Linda's shrill voice filled her car.

"Haley, I need your help. The police found Scott dead in his hotel room. They arrested me this morning. They think I did it!"

Coming soon... *Bent But Not Broken*
Book #2 of The Englewood Medium Series

From the Author

According to www.StalkingAwareness.org, seventy six percent of female homicides by a romantic partner have been stalked beforehand and fifty four percent of those victims reported the stalking to police before they were killed by their stalkers.

A victim of stalking myself, the fear was so intense that I waited almost ten years before I could write about it without re-activating the trauma. If you are a victim of stalking, please take the situation seriously and put full measures in place to protect yourself. I ended up leaving my apartment and crossing state lines to be safe. Sometimes, you have to cut your losses and make a drastic change. Nothing is more important than your safety.

Recipes

From *Real Food on a Budget* by Lana McAra

GF Plant-Based Brownies
Prepare Your Plant Ingredients:

Note: I put a whole sweet apple and a medium-size sweet potato into a crockpot and cook them on low overnight. When cool enough to handle, I peel them and put them through a ricer. If you don't have a ricer:

- Peel the apple and dip it into water with a little lemon to prevent browning, then bake, tightly covered until soft enough to make applesauce.
- Bake the sweet potato, then cool and peel.

When ready to bake your brownies, set the oven to 375° and grease a brownie pan or 9 x 9 cake pan.

Dry Ingredients
- ¼ Cup any gluten-free flour, such as rice flour or almond flour (Coconut flour is very dry and might make the brownies dry. Since I'm not gluten-free, I use all-purpose flour and the result turns out fine.)
- 2 Tablespoons cornstarch or arrowroot powder
- ½ teaspoon salt of your choice
- 1 teaspoon baking soda

Set aside Dry Ingredients.

Wet Ingredients:

- cooked apple, cooled
- cooked sweet potato, cooled
- ½ Cup coconut oil (or a soft, ripe avocado)
- ¼ Cup agave or honey, can use less to taste
- 1 teaspoon vanilla extract

In a large mixing bowl, beat all of the above ingredients well with a mixer. When creamy add:

- ½ Cup cocoa powder (use Special Dark cocoa if you like robust chocolate flavor)

Beat until creamy, then add:

- 4 eggs, one at a time, beating well to a creamy texture after each egg

Using a rubber spatula, dust the Dry Ingredients over the Wet Ingredients and turn gently until thoroughly mixed. If the batter is too wet, add a bit more flour. If it's too dry, add a bit of water. Since you're using whole foods, the dryness and wetness will be different each time. The results, however, will always be delicious. Makes 9 luscious brownies.

Haley's Beef Stew

Part 1: The night before:

To your crockpot, add in this order:

- 1 medium onion, quartered
- 2 ribs of celery with the leaves left on, cut into 2" lengths
- 2-inch wedge of fresh cabbage
- 1-2 lb. stew beef or lamb
- 1 beef bouillon cube or 1 teaspoon beef soup base

- 1 teaspoon season salt
- ¼ teaspoon black pepper
- 3 quarts of water

Set the crockpot to high and cook all night, turning to low in the early morning hours. Add water to bring the broth's level up to half full, if needed, and simmer until ready to assemble the stew in Part 2.

Note: Part 1 is very forgiving. If you set the crockpot at 8 p.m. and wake up at midnight, check it for water level and turn it to low. If you sleep through until 9 a.m., do the same. The broth needs time to meld flavors, so if you add water, allow an hour for the broth to blend.

Part 1 can be cooled and put into the fridge overnight before beginning Part 2, if you can't finish it the same day.

Part 2: Serving Day

Remove all meat from the crockpot and set aside.

Put the veggies into a blender or food processor and add enough broth to cover. If your family likes veggies, pulse a few times to break up the large pieces. My family has several veggie-haters, so I blend until smooth. Return all the broth to the crockpot and set to high.

Note: If you're in a hurry, use a Dutch oven in the oven set at 350° for two hours.

Add to the broth:

- 8 medium potatoes, peeled and quartered
- 2 carrots, cut into 1-inch cubes (I use half a bag of baby

carrots when I'm pressed for time.)
- top off with the cooked stew meat, broken into bite-size pieces
- add water, if needed, to barely cover the meat

Taste for seasoning. Cook until tender but not mushy, 8 hours on low or 4 hours on high.

Before serving: thicken the broth by mixing:
- ¼ Cup water
- 2 Tablespoons of flour or cornstarch

Stir briskly until the lumps are gone. While the broth is bubbling, slowly pour the flour mixture through a small strainer directly into the stew. Stir using a fork or wire whip, using gentle movements. Let bubble for 5-10 minutes, stirring a few times, carefully so the potatoes don't break up. Serves 8. The leftovers are amazing.

Mashed Potato Rolls

With a mixer, beat together in a large bowl:

- 1 Cup hot mashed potatoes (can be leftover mashed potatoes)
- 2 Tablespoons fat, such as bacon grease, lard, butter or coconut oil
- 2 Tablespoons sugar to help the yeast grow
- 1½ teaspoons salt

Beat until smooth.
- Add 1 egg and beat until smooth

Beat in:
- 4 Cups of cool liquid, such as reserved water from

cooking the potatoes, milk or water
- 1 pkg (1 Tablespoon) yeast

Beat until smooth.

- Add 2 Cups of bread flour

Beat for 5 minutes. Using a wooden spoon, mix in 2-3 cups additional flour until the dough leaves the sides of the bowl. Turn out the dough to a floured surface and knead a few times to create a smooth surface. Cover with plastic wrap or a small overturned bowl.

Wash the mixing bowl and dry well. Coat the bowl with oil and return the dough to the bowl, turning the dough to coat with oil. Cover with the plastic wrap touching the dough and a tea towel over the top of the bowl. Let rise until doubled, about 30 minutes.

Pinch off sections of dough about the size of a ⅓-cup measure. Fold in the edges to form a smooth top and arrange in a well-greased 9 x 13 pan to make about 24 rolls. Pierce the top of each roll with a fork to eliminate internal bubbles. Let rise for 30 minutes,

Bake at 350° until golden, about 35 minutes. Test for doneness by lifting the top of a center roll with a fork. The center should be flaky. When done, immediately brush the tops with butter. Makes about 2 dozen rolls.